Pucking Billionaire

Misha Bell

♠ Mozaika Publications ♠

Published by Mozaika Publications, an imprint of Mozaika LLC.
www.mozaikallc.com

Cover by Najla Qamber Designs
www.qamberdesignsmedia.com

ISBN: 978-1-63142-891-3
Paperback ISBN: 978-1-63142-903-3

Chapter 1

Sophia

"He left me *everything*?" I stare at Mr. Cohen, my late father's lawyer, like he's about to sprout pink squirrels from his eyeballs.

I thought my father would leave me some photographs, or my grandmother's ring, or a creepy doll that comes to life at night. Not all his earthly possessions. Of which there were apparently many.

"Your father was an orphan and an only child." Mr. Cohen gestures around his drab office as if answers might be written on one of the many degrees decorating the beige walls. "Whom did you expect to be in his will?"

I shrug. His new wife? Their kids, if they had any? Certainly not the daughter who'd refused to see him her whole life until a month ago. Even then, we'd only met once for a super-awkward lunch before he ghosted me. Or so I thought. Turns out he'd passed... and, for all I know, is an actual ghost now, watching us in this very room.

Okay, that was in poor taste. Just goes to show I probably shouldn't be in his will. Hell, I didn't even go to his funeral because I barely knew the guy, and I'm not good with death-related things.

"I've known Theodore since before you were born," Mr. Cohen says softly. "He truly cared about you."

"Then why wasn't he in my life?" I ask bitterly.

It's a topic we danced around during our one and only meeting, but my father kept steering the conversation toward me and my studies, so I never got any sort of real answers.

Mr. Cohen sighs. "Your mother had full custody of you and didn't allow Theodore anywhere near you. She even got a restraining order—completely unnecessarily, I should add."

"What? No! That can't be true." There's so much to unpack there that I don't even know where to start. "My mother is a drug addict," I say. "I'm pretty sure she was back then too. How could she get custody over a wealthy father?"

Mr. Cohen shrugs. "Theodore wasn't particularly wealthy back then, and judges often have a bias in favor of the mother. Your father knew Eleni was an addict, but she somehow passed her court-mandated drug testing. Then she twisted her history with your father to make him seem controlling and abusive. All of his attempts to get her help were made out to be examples of his controlling nature. She claimed he tricked her when he brought her to America from Greece, and that his ultimate goal was to separate her from her friends and family back there, so he could isolate her and keep her under his thumb. None of it was true, of course, but—"

"But she doesn't have any friends or family in Greece," I say, latching on to the most glaring discrepancy.

At least that's what my mother told me, back when we were on speaking terms.

Mr. Cohen nods. "I'm not surprised. She told many lies during the court proceedings, lies that hurt your father both personally and professionally. It took him many years to recover from the damage—both emotional and financial—that your mother inflicted on him."

My head is spinning. Lies. So, so many lies. My mother told me that my father was awful. That he abandoned us for his other family. But clearly, there was no other family; otherwise, I wouldn't be here as the sole beneficiary in his will. And the worst thing is, I'm not even particularly surprised to learn any of this.

My mother has always been a manipulative liar. Why did it never occur to me to question her claims about my father?

It's like on some level, I was mad at him for not being there to protect me from her.

"So, anyway," Mr. Cohen says. "As soon as you were old enough, your father tried reaching out to you."

There's a thickness in my throat when I think of all

the times I rebuffed my father, thanks to the poisonous things my mother had told me about him over the years. Things that I'm now realizing are false.

"I'm sorry I wasn't at the funeral," I mutter.

Mr. Cohen waves that away. "Theodore wasn't a religious man. Knowing him, he'd probably say that he was dead at that point, so who cares who showed up? Meeting you at that lunch truly brightened the end of his life, and I know he appreciated that. He told me so."

My eyes water from all the stupid dust permeating this office. "I wish he'd told me that he was sick."

The lawyer looks at me pityingly. "He probably didn't want to burden you."

I bite my lip. "All we talked about was my philosophy degree. Never about him."

"I'm sure he enjoyed hearing about your studies," Mr. Cohen reassures me. "He was paying for them, after all."

I frown at him. "I have a scholarship."

His smile is wan. "You mean the scholarship from the DIBT Foundation?"

I stare at him. "No... Really?"

"I helped your father do all the paperwork. That foundation was created with you in mind."

My drab surroundings suddenly feel surreal. "If he cared about me so much and had that kind of money, why did I grow up so poor?"

Poor is an understatement. I once got a hand-me-down sock from the tooth fairy.

Mr. Cohen shrugs. "He sent exorbitant amounts of money as child support to your mother."

My mother. Of course.

I grit my teeth. This explains so much. Like why Mom was so on edge on my eighteenth birthday. She knew my father's checks, and therefore the drugs, would stop coming in. It must also be why she opened all those credit cards in my name around that time.

Not for the first time, I wonder how different my life would be if I'd managed to crawl out from someone else's birth canal twenty-four years ago. Relatedly, has Mommie Dearest had free will this whole time—and therefore no excuse for her horrible parenting? Or is free will an illusion, in which case I could maybe give her a break?

"Would you like me to read you the will?" Mr. Cohen gently offers.

Huh. Another kind of will. "Sure."

So he does, and as I listen, my head spins—especially when he gets to the part about ten million dollars in my trust fund.

I mean, when we met for the first time, my father did take me to a ritzy restaurant and didn't seem too strapped for cash, but I didn't realize he was a millionaire with a list of possessions longer than my recent thesis on Kant. It's so long that I realize I tuned Mr. Cohen out for a few seconds, and he's still going—which is insane.

"Lastly," Mr. Cohen continues. "He wanted me to make sure you became caretaker of his house in

Westchester, or more specifically, of his beloved turtles that reside there, Donatello and April."

"Turtles?" I blink at Mr. Cohen, wondering if the reading of the will has short-circuited something in my brain.

"Or tortoises," he says. "I'm not sure what the difference is."

"Me neither." What I do know is that Donatello is the name of one of the Teenage Mutant Ninja Turtles, who—as the name implies—aren't tortoises. On the other hand, April is the name of a human reporter who befriends the Ninja Turtles, so, using the skills I learned in a course on logic, it would follow that I might have human wards crashing at my house, and not reptiles.

"Either way, you might want to visit the house soon and meet with your new charges, as well as the staff there. Also, you might want to think about the financial implications of your new situation."

Feeling overwhelmed, I nod.

"Call me if you need anything."

I nod again and stand, knees wobbly.

"Best of luck to you with everything," he says.

In a haze, I turn to leave.

By all rights, I should be happy to have suddenly become rich, but I feel anything but.

Now that I have irrefutable evidence that my father cared about me, I feel terrible that throughout my entire life, I've thought otherwise. If money could buy a time machine, I'd spend any amount to go back and attend my father's funeral. Better yet, I'd tell my younger self to actually get to know him because now I really wish I had, but it's too late.

Also, the money I've just inherited comes with a lot of responsibility that I don't feel prepared for—and I don't just mean Donatello, who may or may not be a turtle who knows ninjutsu, and April, who may or may not be a human female who looks just like Megan Fox. Having always been poor, I worry that I'll somehow end up squandering my newfound inheritance, like some lottery winners do.

Maybe I should take some classes in the personal finance department? Learn about smart investing?

One thing is for certain: for better or worse, my life has forever changed.

Chapter 2

Mason

"Why didn't you finish the deal with Theodore before he passed?" Landon asks.

Thank you, Mr. Fucking Obvious. "I was about to. But then his condition suddenly worsened, so there wasn't an opportunity."

I mean, I guess I could've pushed harder, but Theodore had enough shit to deal with, so I didn't.

"And you think the daughter will work with you?"

"That's why I'm here." I look around the waiting room of the law office and regret doing so instantly.

There's a guy here who's buttoning and unbuttoning his shirt.

So fucking gross. I loathe buttons. They are disgusting, constantly being touched by everyone's fingers and getting swallowed by children who then poop them out—that is, unless they get stuck in their intestines forever.

Looking away, I take a calming breath just as my

therapist taught me. I remind myself that buttons are benign objects. This is merely my koumpounophobia fucking with my brain. It's a rare condition that usually makes you fear buttons, but since I fear nothing, I feel disgust instead.

"At the law office?" Landon clarifies, bringing me back to reality.

"Yeah. I plan to make her an offer." And I'll have to be extra careful to be very civil with the woman, despite how she treated poor Theodore.

Hell, for my team, I'd make a deal with the devil if I had to. This is *that* important to me.

"What a bad idea," Landon says.

"Why?" Irritated, I squeeze my phone in my hand but force myself to relax. This is probably still the fucking buttons pushing my buttons, not Landon.

My hold loosens.

That's better. Just like hockey sticks, phones need a firm grip, not a crushing one—something I learned the hard way by once destroying an iPhone.

Fun fact: If it weren't for koumpounophobia, the iPhone might not even exist. Steve Jobs had the same phobia, and I presume that was why he didn't want buttons on his devices—hence the touch screen.

Landon sighs. "How did you even know where she'd be and at what time?"

My phone case creaks. I guess I'm still not fully over that button sighting—or Landon's annoying self is just getting harder to ignore. "The lawyer is a huge Yetis fan, else I wouldn't have known about the fate of the team."

All it cost me were a few end-of-season tickets.

From the corner of my eye, I spot the man futzing with his shirt again.

Fucker. I wish it were socially acceptable to walk up to a stranger and rip their buttons off.

"And people question *my* emotional intelligence," Landon mutters under his breath.

"I'm about to hang up." By destroying another fucking phone.

When Landon says people question his emotional intelligence, what he probably means is that they compare him to Patrick Bateman, the preppy suit-wearing serial killer from *American Psycho*.

"Just look at this from her perspective," Landon says. "You show up there like some weird stalker and—"

"This is my lawyer's office too. A stalker would wait inside her apartment."

Landon sighs. "She's just lost her father. And she's only learning about the will today. I doubt she'll be in the mood to discuss any sort of business."

As if Landon's words aren't enough of an irritant, the buttons guy is at it again, more vigorously this time.

Why is this okay?

It's grosser than picking out belly button lint in public.

"Oh, please." Despite my best efforts, my voice rises.

"She shunned him all those years, but as soon as he got sick, there she was. You think she was interested in reconciliation? No fucking way. She didn't even come to his funeral. All she wanted was the money, like a gold-digging vulture."

I hear an indignant gasp nearby.

Oh, fuck me.

With a sinking feeling, I follow the sound.

Yep. My plans are fucking toast because there she fucking is—the woman I knew would be here.

The woman I needed to charm so she'd sell me my team.

Chapter 3

Sophia

A minute earlier

Still in a daze, I scan my surroundings.

There are two men waiting here: a mustachioed, portly one reading a magazine and playing with the buttons on the collar of his shirt, and a tall, broody, broad-shouldered specimen who is clutching his phone in a tight fist.

Oh, boy.

That fist.

Not this again.

But yep. There I go, turning wet, hot, and bothered at the mere sight of it.

What is wrong with me? You'd think after all that I've just gone through in that office, sexy times would be the last thing on my mind, but it seems like the stupid fist thing is never turned off.

In reality, I'm a peaceful person—a pacifist, in fact—

and I'm not particularly kinky as far as I can tell, so I don't have a clue why the sight of a man's fist does to me what Viagra would do to a horny male teen. Oh, and the fist being attached to a gorgeous man like this makes the situation infinitely worse.

The guy has piercing gray eyes, a strong—albeit previously broken—nose, a powerful jaw, and eyelashes I'd sell my soul for. And for some reason, he's wearing a track suit, which should make him look like an old-school rapper or mobster. To my eyes, however, he resembles a Viking. Maybe it's the longish blond hair? Or the fierceness he exudes?

If we're asking random questions, how does attraction actually work? Is "being hot" objective or subjective? Do we all have a choice in who we find "hot," or is this just another way to phrase the question about free will?

Whatever. I swallow the excess liquid pooling in my mouth and wish there were a pussy equivalent to swallowing. Just like with fists, despite loathing violence and everything else that Vikings represent, I find them infinitely fascinating. And I'm not proud of this, but I sometimes fantasize about what it would be like to roll in the hay with one... screaming Odin's name as I orgasm.

Fine, maybe I do have a kink. Or two.

"This is my lawyer's office too," the Viking growls sexily. "A stalker would wait inside her apartment."

Who is this "her," and why do I feel jealous?

"Oh, please," the Viking replies to whatever he hears

on the other line, his gray eyes glinting with steel. "She shunned him all those years, but as soon as he got sick, there she was."

Wait a second. Is it my guilty conscience talking, or is he—

"You think she was interested in reconciliation?" he continues. "No fucking way. She didn't even come to his funeral."

Fuck. The brute *is* talking about me. But—

"All she wanted was the money, like a gold-digging vulture."

A gasp escapes my lips and all traces of arousal evaporate, leaving me drier than a prune in the desert.

The asshole Viking makes eye contact with me, and a rollercoaster of emotions flits across his features, not a single one of them guilt for what he said.

Mainly, he seems disappointed that he got caught.

Operating on pure instinct, I close the distance between us, poke his broad chest with my index finger, and hiss, "How dare you?"

Chapter 4

Mason

A few seconds earlier

So, this is Theodore's daughter? She looks like every gold digger that's ever tried to tempt me: tall and slender, with perfectly symmetrical facial features, big breasts, lush chestnut hair, gorgeous brown eyes... and the attitude of a honey badger. The only incongruency is her outfit: instead of high fashion, she's wearing a simple red dress with black polka dots on it, like a sexy ladybug on Halloween. Thankfully, there are no buttons in sight. Gold diggers tend to wear outfits with plenty of those horrible things. This woman also smells differently from most gold diggers I know—who seem to bathe in fancy, nose-tickling perfumes. Instead, I detect juicy mango and mouthwatering watermelon, but that could be my thirst playing tricks.

Eyes narrowing murderously, she rushes at me,

just like Number Twenty did the other day—and he ended up sitting out the rest of that game in the penalty box.

Poking me with her slender finger, she says, "How dare you?"

The urge to lick that finger is strong, which is as dumb of an idea as was talking shit about her where she could overhear me.

"Landon, I'll call you back." I hang up, then stare down at the finger and the woman attached to it. "If you were a guy, you'd lose that appendage."

She draws back, and I realize I'm giving her the look I usually give players of the opposing team on the ice.

Great de-escalation. What's next, spitting at her? Talking shit about her mama? Telling her there are twenty-five polka dots covering her breasts?

"You're a beast." She jerks her finger back and glues her hand to her side, like a gunslinger itching to draw her weapon.

I cock my head. "Is that the best insult you've got?"

On my team, it's the sort of thing we might say to the referee, or to someone's grandmother.

"You're a rabid bear." She looks tempted to poke me with the finger again. "A dumb gorilla."

"Those are just examples of beasts," I can't help but point out.

Why am I antagonizing her when I need her to sell me the team? This is like that time I asked the ref if his wife knew he was fucking us.

"Who the hell are you?" she demands. "How did you know my father?"

Shit. Now she's getting closer to making the stalking accusation I was warned about.

"Theodore owns the hockey team I play on. Owned, I mean."

The reminder that the old man is dead tugs at something in my chest. She, in contrast, doesn't so much as bat an eye.

Gritting my teeth, I continue. "I liked and respected him."

And it's true, I did, though I didn't see him as a father figure like some of the others on the team did. For me, labeling someone a father figure is an insult.

She continues staring at me, so I finish with, "I knew him for many years." It takes effort not to add, "Unlike you."

"Oh." She purses her plump, glossy lips. "I didn't even realize he owned a hockey team."

Of course, she wouldn't know that. She knows nothing about him. But I don't point that out. Instead, I use this as my opening. "He did," I say with a cordiality I usually reserve for talking to ESPN. "He and I were working on a deal where he would sell said team to me, but we didn't finish the paperwork in time..." I look at her meaningfully.

Hopefully, her gold-digging nature will make her more interested in the money than in revenge for my earlier words, which were really just me voicing an unpleasant truth.

Fuck. The deadly stare she gives me is how a ladybug must look at spider mites before devouring them whole—at least that's what I saw in that bug documentary I watched the other day. "Why are you telling me this?" she demands.

"I thought it was obvious," I say, deciding to just go ahead. "I'm here to make a deal with you."

Chapter 5

Sophia

I'm a pacifist.

I abhor violence.

Smacking a man—no matter how much I want to—is an example of violence and therefore would be wrong, both morally and ethically. It would be a bad idea from a practical standpoint as well, seeing that he's huge and dangerous-looking.

"Let me see if I have this straight." I feel proud of myself for using words instead of slaps. "You came here to buy a team I've just inherited?"

He nods. "I'll make it worth your while, believe me."

I snort humorlessly. "Are you completely oblivious to the concept of irony?"

His jaw ticks. "What?"

"A minute ago, you had the balls to call *me* a vulture." He winces as I press on. "The irony is that here *you* are, swooping down right after my father's death, trying to 'make a deal.'" I use my most sarcastic air quotes around the last three words.

"I *am* here to make a deal." He clenches and unclenches his fists, but the sight doesn't turn me on... as much as usual. "A fair deal," he continues as I try to get my breathing under control. "One that's even better than what I would've made with your father."

"Well, then. Considering that I'm a gold digger who only cares about money, I'm about to blow your mind." I channel all my violent fantasies into a single withering look. "I wouldn't sell you a golf club if I were starving and needed money for bread. And in case you're wondering, I don't play golf."

Just like insults, comebacks aren't my strong suit, but this one will have to stand because I'm done talking to this asshole.

I turn to leave, but there's a pained grunt behind me.

I glance back.

The pudgy gentleman I saw earlier is clutching his chest.

What the hell?

He slides out of his chair and sprawls on the floor, eyes closed.

I'm rooted to the spot, in complete shock... but the Viking asshole isn't.

He leaps toward the man, taps his shoulders with both hands, and shouts, "Are you okay?"

No reply.

"He's unresponsive." The Viking meets my gaze. "Phone 911 and get the AED."

The words are said with such commanding force that I find myself running out of the room to comply, only to realize I have no idea what the AED is.

I quickly return and witness my nemesis ripping the man's shirt off of him with one powerful tug, revealing a hairy chest with man boobs. The Viking then puts one of his hands over the other and presses into the man's chest so hard I half expect his ribs to break.

Spotting me, the Viking glares at my empty hands. "Where's the fucking AED? And is the ambulance on the way?"

"What's an AED?" The question comes out in a panicked squeak.

"Useless," the Viking mutters under his breath and stops the compressions to breathe into the fallen man's mouth.

How inappropriate is it that I feel a tiny pang of envy toward the dying man?

"AED stands for automated external defibrillator," says Mr. Cohen as he rushes out of his office. "I'll go get it. You call 911."

"Assuming you can manage that," the Viking says snidely, then resumes the chest compressions, humming what I could swear is "Stayin' Alive" by the Bee Gees.

Frantically fishing out my phone, I dial 911 and tell

the operator what's happened, where I am, and that someone is already performing CPR. I also go into a number of details that might be irrelevant, like why I was here, and what I had for breakfast earlier. Oh, and on top of telling her *my* name, I mention Mr. Cohen and ask the Viking for his.

"Mason," he grumbles. "Mason Tugev, though I have no idea why the 911 operator would care."

"Did you say Tugev?" the 911 operator chirps excitedly. "Like the hockey player?"

Given the mention of a team, I presume yes—and tell her so.

"He's amazing, isn't he?" she says breathlessly.

"Uh-huh. Are the EMTs on the way?"

Mason looks at me questioningly.

"Yes," she says, and I give Mason a thumbs up, which he counters with a frown. "Talking to me doesn't slow them down," the operator continues. "So, please, tell me what Mason Tugev is like in real life?"

I roll my eyes. "Have you seen the film *The Northman*?"

"The one where Eric Northman is a Viking?"

It takes me a second to connect the dots. Eric Northman is a character on *True Blood* played by Alexander Skarsgård, who also plays the berserker in *The Northman*. "Yes," I finally say. "Mason is as friendly as the hero of that movie."

The real-world Mason scowls, proving my point.

"I haven't seen that movie," she says. "Is it good?"

I really hope the EMTs are not delayed by this. "If you like Vikings, it's a must-see."

"Is it about the invention of hockey?" She sounds confused.

Ah. Right. Hockey fan. "No. I doubt the Vikings invented anything apart from horrific ways to execute people. Though they did like to skate and ski."

At this, Mason's frown deepens.

"I think we're getting a little off track," I tell the 911 operator.

And by "off track," I mean the train has grown rockets and is flying to the moon.

"Right," she says sheepishly. "The EMTs will be there in five minutes."

I hang up, just as Mr. Cohen returns with the AED thing, which I realize I've seen before, usually next to a fire extinguisher. I just didn't know what it was.

"Open it," the Viking—I mean, Mason—orders.

Mr. Cohen steps back. "I don't feel comfortable using it on a client."

"Why not?" I ask.

"I could get sued," Mr. Cohen says.

"I'm not a lawyer," Mason says over compressions, "but even I know that there are Good Samaritan laws on the books that protect those who try to help in these circumstances."

Mr. Cohen takes another step back. "The laws you speak of don't protect people as much as everyone thinks they do. I've handled many a case where someone did something grossly negligent, and that term is rather subjective."

I bite my tongue. This is not the time to treat everyone to a philosophical treatise on whether or not we're ethically obligated to help people in need.

Mason looks at me. "Do you have more balls than this coward?"

I nod, even though my heart is hammering. "What do I do?"

Mason sighs. "Open the fucking thing."

I open the AED box, and automated voice prompts start telling me what to do. As instructed, I take out the sticky electrode pads and plug them in. Before I can attach them to the man's body, Mason says, "You need to shave his skin first. There should be a razor in the back of the box."

Shave the man? What's next, a mani-pedi?

But then it clicks. The chest hair is in the way of the electrodes. I rummage for the razor, and there it is.

I attack the hair, but it's too thick and curly. That, or this razor is too dull.

"Take out the child-sized sticky pads," Mason says when he spots my grooming troubles.

I locate the smaller pads and take them out.

"Glue them to where the normal-sized ones would go."

I obey.

"Now rip them off."

I gape at Mason. "Rip?"

"I'm sure you're familiar with waxing," he says. "Same idea."

Oh. Right. I rip off the first pad, removing the stubborn hair and proving without a doubt that our patient isn't faking his unconscious state. Then I do it again on the other spot before attaching the two adult pads to the red, naked patches of skin.

Is the wax thing something I could get sued over? It wasn't negligent, but it was gross.

From here, the AED basically takes over, telling everyone to stay clear when it deems necessary to hit the patient with a shock. Then it tells Mason to resume CPR.

I have to admit, the thing is cool. Kind of like Alexa with a medical degree.

The sound of sirens rings out nearby, followed by the footsteps of firefighters and EMTs. Moving swiftly and determinedly, they relieve Mason, place the patient on a stretcher, and rush away.

As soon as they are gone, I realize I have a question, so I pose it to Mr. Cohen and Mason. "Will he make it?"

"Probably," Mason says. "Then again, there are no guarantees in life."

"Will someone call and tell us?" I wish I'd asked this earlier when I was speaking with the chatty 911 operator.

"Doubt it," Mason says. "It would probably be against HIPAA regulations or some such."

"Well, he's my client," Mr. Cohen says. "So I'll know if he makes it… eventually."

"Will you tell us?" I ask.

"I'd have to ask my client if he would be okay with that," Mr. Cohen says.

I blink at him. "How would he give you permission if he doesn't make it?"

"In that case, I'd ask his family."

"Just don't bother on my account," Mason grumbles.

I turn on him, incredulous. "You don't care?"

"Not particularly," Mason says. "I don't know the man."

"But you saved his life." I glance at Mr. Cohen in the hopes that he can explain the enigma that is Mason.

Mason sighs. "*Maybe* I saved his life. Maybe I didn't. All I wanted was to avoid newspaper headlines that say, 'Hockey player with CPR training watches a man die.'"

It's like he's into two sports: hockey and being an asshole.

"All right," I say. "This was... interesting. I'd better get going."

Apparently, I have a new house to check out and turtles to befriend.

"Wait," Mason says as I turn away. "I want you to consider my deal."

"Sure," I say. "I'll consider it."

With that, I leave without a backward glance.

Just to make sure I'm not a liar, for a millisecond, I consider the idea of selling the team—and decide that my answer is still "hell, no." Even if Mason Tugev weren't such a jerk, I need to wrap my head around my newfound wealth before I make any deals. Also, if I have as much money as Mr. Cohen said, I don't need any more, so I might as well stay diversified by owning a hockey team.

Speaking of diversification and not squandering my inheritance, I need to speak to someone majoring in finance. Which, luckily for me, is my best friend and roommate, Abigail.

Jumping into a cab, I tell the driver to take me home.

Chapter 6

Mason

As soon as Ladybug is gone, I realize I don't have a way to contact her, even if by some miracle she does decide to make a deal.

"You could've handled that better," Cohen says carefully.

In reply, I punch the fucking wall, leaving a big hole in it.

"I'll bill you for that," Cohen says, surprisingly calm. "Oh, and before you ask, I won't be discussing Miss Papachristodoulopoulou with you."

"Papa-what?" I rub my bleeding knuckles.

"Papa-christo-doulo-poulou. It's a common Greek last name."

Sure it is. "Thanks for the culture lesson."

He smirks. "When I invoice you for the wall, I'll also include one billable hour."

"Because that's how long it takes to say that name?"

He shrugs, smirking harder, and I resist the urge to

punch the wall again, deciding to save my emotions for practice.

—————

Usually, I feel at peace after practice, especially when sharing a meal with the team like I am now, but not today.

"So, how did it go?" Jason asks through a mouthful of gyro.

Everyone goes quiet, even the restaurant staff.

My lentil hummus suddenly tastes like packing peanuts. "She didn't sell… yet."

"That fucking sucks," Jason says, and the rest of them echo the sentiment, cursing on my behalf in English, Finnish, Russian, and Canadian French.

"I guessed as much by how vicious you were during the drills," Jason says. "Looks like you'll have to keep eating your cow food for a while longer."

By cow food, he means my extremely nutritious but mostly plant-based diet. "I was going to do that anyway," I mutter. "I eat right to live longer, not just so I can keep playing hockey."

All of my teammates look at me skeptically. The idea of something not being about hockey is as foreign to them as eating a Boston cream doughnut is to me.

Jason wrinkles his nose at my hummus. "If I ate like you, I'd wither away and die."

"I agree with Friday here," Parker butts in. "Except

the order of events would be: fart up a storm and *then* wither away and die."

Jason flicks Parker on the forehead for using the Friday moniker yet again. He's fighting a losing battle, though. Since he was born in a New Jersey township named Voorhees and is a goalie, *Friday the 13ᵗʰ* jokes are as inevitable as stabbings at Camp Crystal Lake.

"Eating lentils all the time doesn't make you fart," I say for what feels like the millionth time. "Your body adjusts."

Some of my teammates nod, but most make fart jokes, like the overgrown children they are. The annoying part is that I know that they know more about nutrition than the average person, being athletes and all. I simply took my diet a step further than needed for hockey by following an eating plan that was lab-tested at Octothorpe. Combined with some prescription medicine and dietary supplements, my diet is meant to slow aging to a crawl, and at thirty-seven years of age, I feel like I'm in my twenties. Still, I will be the first person at this table to retire, and owning this team is the best way to keep these knuckleheads in my life.

"What did the new owner look like?" Jason asks.

"Why?" I ask suspiciously.

He shrugs. "If she's not too hideous, maybe you can convince her to sell the team using your... charms."

The rest of the team make sounds reminiscent of a pack of horny hyenas.

"She's not unattractive," I say grudgingly. "But I

doubt she'd want to have anything to do with my charms, even if they were the last charms on Earth."

And the feeling is mutual.

"Not unattractive?" Jason squeezes his gyro until tzatziki sauce drips onto his lap. "Maybe I should help a brother out, with my 'charms.'"

"Fuck no." I almost punch his face to punctuate the point, then check myself just in time because what the fuck is wrong with me?

Everyone stops eating and stares at me in confusion.

Jason cocks his head. "You like her?"

He and the rest of the team have been trying to get me laid for a month now, but I've been practicing celibacy.

Do I like Ladybug?

The idea is absurd.

I haven't liked anyone for a while now, and if I were going to end that streak, it wouldn't be with a disagreeable gold digger. Also, she's way too young.

"Oh, I get it," Jason says to everyone conspiratorially. "He can't act on it because she owns the team. If he tapped that, and then they broke up, things would get pretty bad."

I can't believe he says "tap that" unironically. Also, unbelievably, the idiot makes a good point—like a stopped clock that's right twice a day. Not that I needed his point to avoid Ladybug the way an aphid would her insect namesake.

"Can we talk about anything else?" I imbue the

question with enough threat to make sure everyone knows that if they push, their face will resemble that wall in the lawyer's office.

"Sure," Jason says with an impish grin. "Seen any new nature documentaries lately?"

I groan. I let him share my Netflix account, and this is the thanks I get. He must have spied on my Recently Watched, which are all nature documentaries because they help me relax.

"Sure, I saw one about ladybugs," I say with a straight face. If I don't show them that it bothers me, the teasing will subside more quickly. Hopefully. "They're carnivorous and therefore a natural insecticide, which is why they're considered a lucky charm all over the globe."

With loud snore sounds, Jason drops his head toward his plate, stopping only an inch away from it. "Shit. That was so boring I fell asleep."

"You should repeat what you just said, but in the voice of David Attenborough," Parker says.

"If you know who David Attenborough is, you must've seen your own share of nature documentaries," I point out.

"No, I haven't," Parker replies, a bit too quickly. "Also, it's *Sir* David Attenborough."

I grin as the ribbing turns Parker's way—with everyone insisting he call them sir also, followed by more nonsense.

I sigh. My teammates are like my brothers, for better or for worse. When it counts, we have each other's backs and wouldn't tease about something real, like my button thing. In fact, no one has said anything, but I've noticed they've started wearing buttonless tracksuits when I'm around, even when we go out to fancy clubs.

Fuck. If I don't buy the team, I'm going to let them down. What if she makes changes that impact us for the worse? Or—

"When are you going to talk to her again?" Jason asks, bringing me back to the matter at hand.

"No idea," I say. "First, I need a game plan."

———

As soon as I step into my apartment, my cat, Spike, runs over and greets me with an enthusiasm you'd expect from a golden retriever puppy.

"I'm happy to see you too," I say gruffly before heading into the kitchen to feed him a few slices of sashimi-grade tuna.

Next, I grab a bottle of my favorite vodka and videocall Evan, my buddy from Florida. We have a mutually beneficial arrangement to not let the other drink alone.

"Hey," Evan says, then frowns at the bottle in my hands. "I'm sorry, I quit drinking."

"You did?"

"I have a kid around now," Evan says. "Don't want to set a bad example."

Ah. Right. "Makes sense."

"You should quit, too," Evan suggests. "It doesn't fit your healthy eating schtick."

"Actually, back in Estonia, vodka is believed to cure all sorts of ailments." When I was a kid, whenever I was sick, my mom would dip my socks in vodka and have me put them on, so I'd smell like an alcoholic when I got to school.

Fuck. Now I need that drink all the more. This happens whenever I think back to my family and how they've cut all ties with me.

"Weren't you born in the US?" Evan asks.

I shrug. "My Estonian-born parents still managed to pass on their vodka beliefs to me." And their obsession with saunas, which I got the whole team into.

"Well, I'm pretty sure the science on it isn't great," Evan says. "So if you're avoiding doughnuts, you might want to avoid vodka too."

"You know what? Next time I don't want to drink by myself, I'll head over to a bar instead of calling you and getting a lecture."

"Perfect," he says. "That way, maybe you'll finally meet a woman who—"

I end the call.

Why does everyone who starts dating want me to join their cult? Similarly with people who have children: they turn into walking PR campaigns for spawning.

I eye the vodka and debate breaking the drink-by-myself taboo.

No. I guess some things I learned from my parents are too difficult to ignore.

Fine.

I put the vodka away and videocall Coach, the person in my life who simultaneously serves as a therapist, priest, and probation officer.

"Hey, kid." Coach strokes his record-breaking beard. "Or should I call you Boss?"

"I'm not your boss… yet."

"What happened?" Coach mindlessly tugs on his beard—or as Jason would say, "looks for a snack in it."

I tell Coach what happened, and when I get to the CPR part of the story, he compliments me on my life-saving skills, and he might as well be patting himself on the back since he's the one who suggested that I learn first aid.

He tosses his beard over his shoulder. "Maybe you should consider my other suggestion?"

"No." I can't believe he's bringing it up again. Despite the beard making him look practically ancient, Coach is only ten years older than I am, yet he's got it into his head that he should retire—provided he finds a suitable replacement first. Why on earth he thinks I'm capable of filling his sasquatch-sized shoes is beyond me.

Our team is one of the few in the league that doesn't have a captain, but if we did, I wouldn't even be that. I don't have it in me to be all rah-rah inspirational. In fact, I've been accused of the opposite.

The words "pessimist" and "cynical" have been thrown around a lot in my vicinity.

The beard twitches in a way that suggests that Coach might be pursing his never-visible lips. "In that case, try again with the new owner. Maybe be cordial next time."

"Yeah. Thanks. Great advice. Why didn't I think of that?"

His eyes narrow. "Sarcasm is the lowest form of wit."

"Puns are lower. And fart jokes." Along with the other things that come out of Jason's mouth.

"Be that as it may, my advice stands," Coach huffs. "Keep your temper in check. It's a good idea on the ice, if you become a coach, and really, as a human being in general."

Great. He's in one of *those* moods. "I'll be nicer to her next time. I promise." It will be a huge challenge, but the team is worth it.

"Great." He scratches where his chin might be hiding. "Now, I have to go. Wife wants a foot rub."

"TMI," I say and hang up, but with a reluctant smile.

Coach has found himself a unicorn: a happy marriage.

Pretty sure in all of New York, that's him and one other guy.

I pace around my place while Spike, channeling a circus cat, glides between my feet. The thing I'm pondering is: how do I take another stab at talking to Ladybug?

Step one: I need to find her. I doubt Cohen will help me again, so I'm on my own this time.

Speaking of Cohen, thanks to him, I know her last name now, even if I wouldn't dare try to say it out loud: Papachristodoulopoulou. Her first name—Sophia—I know from Theodore.

I head over to my laptop and google that combo.

Nope. There's an alpine skier named Sophia Papamichalopoulou, but that's not Ladybug. Something else I learn is that her last name means "descendant of the priest and servant of Christ." Huh. Another search later, I discover that unlike their Roman Catholic counterparts, Greek Orthodox priests are allowed to marry, which can lead to pretty long last names for their descendants.

Put another way, I find out nothing.

Hmm. She looked to be in her early twenties, so it's a good bet that she'll be on TikTok.

Nothing comes up. Weird.

Snapchat?

Still no. Same goes for Facebook.

Not into social media? I guess that's one thing we have in common.

Fine. Plan B—which will make me even more of a stalker.

I dial Landon and make a point to not use video so that I don't have to see his smug "I told you so" expression when he learns how much of a mess I've made.

"Let me guess," he says instead of a hello. "Was it *her* who said, 'How dare you?'"

"It was. You were right. Can we move on?"

"Hell fucking no," he says. "Tell me what happened."

I do so, feeling sick of the story already.

"Is she hot?" he asks.

"What?" I'm squeezing my phone too hard again.

"She sounded hot," he says. "All breathy and indignant."

I clench and unclench my free hand. "What she looks like is irrelevant."

"Is it?" he asks.

Great. Another one. If he asks me to convince her with my "charms," I'll introduce him to Jason so they can braid each other's pubes.

"I need your help," I grit out through clenched teeth.

"Obviously you do," he says. "So much help that you'll have to be more specific."

My fucking phone case is creaking again. "You have a guy who can find information on people. I want him to make a dossier on her."

Silence.

"You there?" I growl.

"Yeah, I just can't believe my ears. Two seconds ago, you said that I was right when I called you a stalker. Now, instead of changing your ways, you're doubling down on it."

"What choice do I have?"

He sighs. "Wait till she meets with you and the team? She *is* the new owner."

"Fuck, no. If you don't want to help, that's fine, but I—"

"I'm texting you the guy's info," he says, and I can somehow hear the eyeroll over the line. "I'll also tell him to expect to hear from you."

"Thanks. I owe you one."

"It's nothing. Just tell me how it all goes."

I grudgingly promise that I will and hang up. Then I get in touch with the guy, whose name is Max Stolyar, and pay his exorbitant rate. Max reassures me that no, he doesn't charge per syllable in the query's name, and that he'll have something for me in a few hours.

To bide my time, I turn on the TV and put on the next nature documentary from my very long to-watch list.

The show takes place in the ocean, which would usually be calming as fuck, but the unresolved Ladybug situation is bugging me too much to enjoy anything at the moment.

Finally, after what feels like a year of waiting, I get a text from Max.

Chapter 7

Sophia

"Honey, I'm home." I step into the tiny studio that I share with my bestie and bump right into our bunk bed.

"What's with the racket?" Abigail mutters grumpily from the top bunk, the "high station" she received by literally drawing a short straw when we first moved into this glorified doll house. "People are trying to sleep."

I look at the clock on our dingy little microwave, or as I call it, our micro-microwave. "It's 3:45 in the afternoon."

"So? I was cramming for Financial Calculus all night," Abigail retorts. "And now I need the sleep to consolidate my memory."

"See? This is why philosophy is a much better major," I say with a grin. "There's no such thing as Philosophical Calculus and therefore no need for sleepless nights."

"Sure, if by 'a much better major,' you mean the peace of mind that comes with knowing you're completely unemployable." She swings her long, perfectly shaped legs off the bunk bed. "Also, isn't there Ethical Calculus? Felicific Calculus?"

Should I argue that I *will* be able to find a job? No. Instead, and not for the first time, I marvel at how incredibly smart Abigail is. She's just schooled me on my own area of study, because yes, those types of calculus do exist. Our school just doesn't offer them as courses, and if it did, I'd probably avoid them like a carrot would a bunny.

"Let me make you some breakfast." I step over to the minifridge, pull out a frozen burrito, and pop it into the micro-microwave.

"Thanks." Abigail climbs down from the bunk bed and walks over to the toilet—yes, the one in the middle of the room. "Don't turn around," she warns.

As per our usual protocol, I not only avoid turning but also sing "Let It Go" from *Frozen* loudly enough to drown out any unladylike sounds that might come out of my roommate.

"Done." She punctuates the word with a flush. "Oh, and you need to update your repertoire."

I ignore that. Whenever it's my turn, she exclusively sings "Ring of Fire" by Johnny Cash, which makes me think of herpes, chlamydia, and Chipotle.

I move out of her way so she can use our kitchen/bathroom sink, one that serves as an

impromptu shower on days when we don't have time
to swing by the locker rooms at our school's gym.

By the time the micro-microwave beeps, Abigail
deems herself presentable, and I agree. Even without
makeup and after sleep deprivation, she's gorgeous:
blonde, tall, toned, naturally pouty-lipped, and with
fierce blue eyes. Put another way, she strongly
resembles Lagertha from *Vikings*.

"So." She grabs the burrito and bites off a huge
chunk of it. "How did it go?" Her question sounds
muffled by half-chewed rice and beans.

I stick another burrito into the micro-microwave—
a dessert version that I like, with chocolate, peanut
butter, and jelly, that has about the amount of sugar it
takes in treats to teach an elephant to ride a unicycle. "I
think I'm rich."

She nearly chokes on her food and then demands all
the details. When I tell her all the events of today, she's
disturbingly more interested in the Viking than in my
new wealth. Offhandedly, I mention his name. She
audibly swallows her food and gasps. "Did you say
Mason Tugev?"

"Yeah." I didn't realize assholes like him were
household names.

"The hockey player?"

I roll my eyes. "Yeah. I just told you that."

"You know he's a billionaire, right?" she squeals.
"And you told him 'no deal.'"

He is? "I thought professional athletes made
millions, not billions."

"Ah, but this one used the money from his contract to invest in Octothorpe. Early." She digs out her phone and taps at it a few times. "I just sent you an article from WSJ."

WSJ? Does that stand for Whippersnapper Scallywag Jamboree? More importantly: "Isn't Octothorpe the place you're dying to work at?"

She nods with such enthusiasm she almost pecks the burrito with her nose. "Everything that company touches turns to gold. Oh, and they still give out stock options to their employees."

"Everything turning to gold didn't work out so well for King Midas," I remind her.

She nods sagely. "You're talking about his troubles jerking off?"

I snort. "Yeah. I think that's also the backstory behind Goldmember from *Austin Powers*."

The micro-microwave dings.

"Read the article," she says as I fish out my burrito.

I pull out my phone, and as I chew, I find out that a) WSJ stands for *The Wall Street Journal* and b) Mason Tugev is the best player in the DHL—the Diamond Hockey League, which has zero connection to the shipping company with the same name. Mason first became famous when he refused to leave his team, even when a more famous team tried to poach him. Then his fame grew when he kept playing hockey even after making an obscene amount of money, which leads to the all-important point c) he is indeed a billionaire, thanks to "shrewd investing."

Hmm.

I look up from my phone. "Do you think he wants the hockey team because he knows it's about to go up in price?"

Abigail shakes her head. "Sports teams appreciate over the long term. He might want the prestige of owning a team. Or is looking for tax benefits."

I chew the burrito and ponder the kinds of yummy foods I can now afford. Caviar? Truffles? Godiva chocolates?

"So," Abigail says as my stomach rumbles. "The most important part: what did he look like?"

I have no idea why, but I blush like a medieval nun upon meeting a half-naked Viking.

She grins. "That hot, huh?"

"He was rude and obnoxious."

She waves that off. "Does he have any ink?"

Now it's my turn to grin. When it comes to men, tattoos are Abigail's Achilles heel... made out of kryptonite. She'd date—and I use that term loosely— any loser with a nice picture on his skin for her to gawk at, even a telemarketer who cold-calls people early in the morning to sell them fidget spinners.

"No tattoos," I say. "None that were visible anyway." But damn her, she's got me wondering what he looks like under that track suit.

"No ink is good," she says. "Given that he's yours, and I don't want the temptation."

"Can we have a serious talk for a moment?" I ask, my burrito suddenly losing its sweetness.

She cocks her head.

I pull out the papers listing all my inherited stuff. "How can I make sure not to squander all this new money?"

Abigail snatches the papers and reads carefully, forehead furrowing.

A couple of times, she whistles, which must be a good sign.

After a few minutes, she hands me the papers back, eyes shining. "You're super rich. The kind of rich where it would be a serious challenge to squander it all."

I sigh. "I don't want to take on that challenge. Quite the opposite."

She nods. "I think I can give you a few pointers. Let me have a think."

"You're the best." I grin at her. "Tomorrow at the cafeteria, lunch is on me."

Abigail tsk-tsks with mock disapproval. "Already squandering money on luxuries, are we?"

"Yeah. I'm also taking a cab to see my new house— and my new turtles."

———

My new house isn't a house.

It's a mansion, and I don't use that word lightly. It's like if the Downton Abbey home impregnated the White House, and then severely overfed the resulting baby. The mansion is surrounded by countless acres of perfectly maintained gardens, a big chunk of which are covered by a see-through dome—making it the biggest greenhouse I've ever seen.

"Are you expected?" the cab driver asks when we approach the tall, ornate gate.

"This place is mine," I say with uncertainty. "But... I don't know."

With a confused expression, he pulls up to the intercom that's right next to the gate and rolls down my window.

I press the button.

"Hello," a posh female voice says with a British accent. "How can I be of help?"

"Hi. This is Sophia Papa—"

"Ah, Mistress Papachristodoulopoulou," the woman says. "Please come inside."

I gape at the intercom. That was the closest anyone has ever gotten to pronouncing my last name correctly, and the first time anyone has called me a mistress.

"You want to get out here?" the cab driver asks.

Is he joking? The driveway is a mile long. "Please take me to the front door."

He does so, and as I pay, a woman in her late twenties runs to the cab to get the door for me.

I climb out and try not to gape at her. She's wearing a lot of black leather, has more piercings than a pincushion, and is covered in so many tattoos that, if she were a dude, she'd have a hall pass into Abigail's vagina.

"Thanks," I tell her and examine the mansion, which looks even bigger up close.

"No problem, Mistress Papachristodoulopoulou," the tattooed chick says in the same British accent I heard at the gate. "Welcome."

"Thank you," I say. "Please call me Sophia."

"But, of course... Mistress Sophia," she says.

"Just Sophia," I say and don't add that, out of the two of us, she's the one who looks a lot more like a mistress... of the BDSM kind.

"All right." She wrinkles her nose so hard her nostril piercing clanks against the bull ring. "In that case, call me Euphemia."

"Euphemia." Should I tell her that means "well-spoken" in Greek?

"Or Effie," she says, nose wrinkling again with a louder clank. "If you'd prefer."

"Nice to meet you... Effie. What do you do here?"

Her spine goes rod straight. "I'm the Butler... Mistress."

"Call me Sophia." And did she say butler?

"Pardon me," she says. "Addressing an employer in a respectful way was drilled into me back at butler school."

So she actually is the butler. "The word Mistress is respectful?" For me, it brings to mind whips, chains, and homewreckers.

"But of course it is," she says. "It is, after all, the feminine form of Mister."

I guess that makes sense. "Did my father like to be so formal?"

She shakes her head. "He made me call him Theo, so you didn't fall all that far from that apple tree."

Why does that make me feel warm and fuzzy? "What do you do as a butler?"

My only exposure to her profession is Alfred, Batman's surrogate father figure.

"I prepare rooms, host guests, tidy up, order goods for the household, make calls for—"

She goes on for a while, and it sounds more and more like a job interview, or job justification. Is she worried that I'll bring my own butler? Or—and this would be totally crazy, I know—that I'll manage without a butler?

"Anyway," she finally says. "I can give you a more detailed outline of my duties at your leisure. In the meanwhile, I imagine you'd like an introduction to the rest of the staff, along with a tour."

"A tour would be nice." As would knowing how many people work at this place. I don't ask that, though, because it sounds like something I should already know.

As we walk the spacious grounds, there is a definite motif emerging—that of turtles. There are paintings of turtles, statues of turtles, murals depicting turtles, ceramic plates with turtles on them, and realistic photograms of every type of turtle known to man. When we get to "the media room," which is really a private movie theater, a film about turtles is looping on the giant screen.

"At least it's all consistent," I mutter under my breath.

Effie smiles but just with her eyes, which must be a butler thing. "In the library, ninety percent of the books are about tortoises."

I grin. "Of course. I bet turtle-themed music is playing somewhere in the house as we speak."

Effie betrays her profession because a genuine smile actually touches her pierced lips. "If it had been up to Theo, ancient Hindus would be correct about Earth being flat and resting on the back of a large turtle."

My grin widens. "A turtle that stands on an even larger turtle, which stands on top of an even larger turtle —with turtles all the way down." We talked about this idea in one of my classes as an example of infinite regress.

Effie nods. "If this place had a motto, it would be 'turtles all the way down.'"

I wonder if my father was this into turtles when he met my mother. She certainly never mentioned it, and it seems like the sort of thing you ought to mention. Maybe turtles were his way to cope with what she put him through? No idea, and at this point, it's like asking what came first, the turtle or the egg.

"The staff are in the reading room," Effie says and gestures toward a door, her smile disappearing.

I follow her in, and I meet three older ladies—who surprisingly look nothing like turtles—and I learn that they share the cooking, cleaning, gardening, and other responsibilities with Effie.

The tour continues in that vein, and when we enter the garage, I can't help but whistle.

The cars my father left me are worth a fortune. There are representatives from Bugatti, Ferrari, Bentley, and—in case I ever wondered if my father had a mid-life crisis—a Porsche. Of course, no car collection would be complete without a green Volkswagen Beetle made to look like a giant turtle.

"This is Richard," Effie says.

A car-turtle named Richard? No, she's pointing at a short gentleman who seems to be fixing the car-turtle, or feeding it.

"Hello, Miss Papa-can-you-hear-me-lou," Richard says to me with a wide grin. "You look just like the late Theo."

Effie frowns. "I told you. It's Papachristodoulopoulou."

"My bad," he says. "Papa-can-you-find-me-in-the-night-Christ-dual-transmission-Paula-lou."

Effie looks at me apologetically. "I had everyone practice. I swear."

I grin. "I've heard worse." I turn to Richard. "Please call me Sophia."

Adults don't usually jump up and down in glee, but Richard does. "Nice to meet you, Sophia. Call me Dick."

Hmm. "All right... Dick."

"Or Dickie," he says.

Must I?

"No, call him Richard," Effie says with a frown that brings her eyebrow piercings perilously close together.

He sighs. "Yeah. Everyone calls me Richard in the household."

Why is he upset about that fact? If my name were shortened to Pussy and had a diminutive form like Pus, I'd go by the full name, always. Then again, as Shakespeare famously put it, "A rose by any other name is just as sweet," so even if my name were shortened to Pussy, I'd still smell like—

"Let's continue the tour," Effie says, turning on her stiletto heel.

"Wait." Richard thrusts a business card into my hand. "Whenever you need a ride, let me know."

Wow. I have a personal driver? And to think I felt like I was splurging when I took that cab ride over here.

"I'll be the best driver you've ever had," Richard calls after me as we head toward the exit. "You'll see!"

Yeah, sure, just like this mansion is the best I've ever owned.

"Thanks!" I turn to wave at Richard as we leave the garage. "Where are we going now?" I ask Effie once we're heading down a large corridor.

"I've saved the best for last," she says.

"Oh?"

She opens a set of French doors that lead into the giant greenhouse I saw earlier. "It's about time you meet Donatello, April, and Dr. Kelpcon."

Hold up, there are three turtles now? Also, why name the third one Dr. Kelpcon? That doesn't sound like a TMNT character. Unless that was one of the minor villains? Actually, it sounds more like a convention for people who like to eat kelp.

My thoughts are interrupted by a weird noise coming from behind the tall shrubs nearby. It sounds like rhythmic moans and thumps. The moans are pained, like how I feel when I wake up hungover, especially if that happens to coincide with my period. Also, there's a sound of something heavy and hard rubbing against something else heavy and equally hard, like two tanks cuddling.

Effie must hear all this too because she frowns. "Maybe I should show you another part of the estate. The turtles seem to be busy at the moment."

Nope. I'm morbidly curious now, so I pick up my pace until I clear the shrubs and see the source of the noise… and kind of wish I'd taken Effie's offer.

A giant turtle is mounting another giant turtle from the back, and it's as hilarious as it is intimidating. He—I presume—is using an appendage that is more like a tentacle from anime porn than a penis. It's longer than his very long neck, and he is fully dedicated to the act, thrusting much faster than you'd expect from such a famously slow creature. He must love this too, because his reptilian mouth is open wide, and there's drool dripping onto the shell of the female—again, I presume the gender.

I stare at them, speechless, and not just because I'm witnessing the literal meaning of "drooling over you."

"Yes! Just like that," shouts a woman in a white coat, making me notice her for the first time. "You're doing an amazing job, Don! You're almost there. Keep giving it to her. Hard."

All right, I had my pronouns correct.

Don—which must be short for Donatello—appears encouraged because his moans grow louder and his drool more plentiful.

Effie angrily clears her throat.

The woman in the white coat glares at the butler. "Hush," she hisses. "Don is about to ejaculate into April."

Okay, I'm not one to kink-shame but—

Just then, Don reaches an orgasm—or again, so I assume—with a sound that will forever haunt me. As he slowly moves off April, I find myself worried that she didn't enjoy the experience. Unlike Don, she was pretty Zen through the whole thing. Also, I wonder if turtles—or any animals—can fall in love, and therefore can be said to have "made love?" For that matter, can they consent to sex, the way humans do? If—

"Good job," the woman in the lab coat says boisterously, interrupting my philosophical musings. She turns to Effie. "Now you can speak."

"I'm here to introduce you to Mistress Papachristodoulopoulou," Effie says sternly. "You know, the person who now pays for all this." She gestures around the habitat.

The other woman seems to notice me for the first time. "You're Theo's daughter?"

I nod. "You must be Dr. Kelpcon."

"Call me Acadia." She extends her rubber-gloved hand.

"I'm Sophia." I shake the hand cautiously, praying it wasn't utilized to assist the turtles with the mating in any way.

"It's a pleasure to meet you," Acadia says. "And if you're free at the moment, I'd like to tell you all the reasons you should keep the breeding program going."

I cock my head. "Breeding program?" Please, pretty please, let this be about turtles and only turtles.

Acadia blinks at me. "You don't know about the program?"

"Not everyone's life revolves around the tortoises," Effie says sternly.

"That's true," Acadia says, and it's clear she means "but it should." She turns back to me. "Your father made it his personal goal to bring this rare species of tortoise back from the brink of extinction." She looks lovingly at Romeo—I mean, Donatello—who is now blissfully grazing on the nearby grass. "Don has personally sired two hundred and seventy offspring."

"That sounds like a lot," I say.

"It's a start," Acadia says. "We need the population to reach over fifteen hundred."

"That is a lot of turtles doing the beast with two backs," I say with a grin. "And two carapaces."

"Tortoises," Acadia corrects in a professorial tone.

Oh. "What's the difference?"

"Turtles live in the ocean, while tortoises live exclusively on land. Turtles are usually omnivores, while tortoises are mostly herbivores. The shells of—"

I tune the rest of it out, as I've been doing with other minutia lately, because I'm worried the extra info might push one of the philosophy-related terms from my brain before finals. All I know is, the Ninja Turtles must really be turtles because they eat pizza with chicken and pepperoni, so they're omnivores all the way.

At some point mid-lecture, Effie butts in to say that we have some important business back at the mansion.

"Ah," Acadia says. "I guess I'll go over the basics of testudines another time."

Testudines? Basics? I feel like I could take what she's talked about thus far and turn it into a biology dissertation.

When we get back into the mansion, I ask Effie what the important business is.

"Oh, I just wanted to save us from a day-long lecture."

"Thanks," I say. "Now if you don't mind, I want to wander around a bit."

She bows. "It's your house."

And so it is, which is why I examine everything, each nook, cranny, and turtle depiction, feeling increasingly overwhelmed as I do.

Before coming here, I wasn't sure what to do with my wealth, but now I also don't know what to do with this mansion. There are people depending on me for their income, so if I mismanage my money, they'll lose their livelihood. Oh, and a cherry on top of that guilt cake would be a species going extinct, and Donatello becoming a very sad tortoise without all that nookie.

My phone dings.

It's a text from Abigail:

Lunch at 2?

I reply in the affirmative and hope that she's ready to set me on a righteous financial path.

Returning to the garage, I make Richard's day by asking him to give me a ride to school.

———

"Turtle sex?" Abigail nearly chokes on her California roll.

"*Tortoise* sex," I correct with a smirk. "There's a huge difference."

"Right, one longer than his neck."

"Let's please *not* talk about tortoise cock." I put a piece of my roll into my mouth and resist cringing. I'm not a food snob, by any means, but college cafeteria sushi is to regular sushi what granola bars are to deep-fried Oreos.

"Got it. No *tortoise* cock," Abigail says. "Have you heard from Mason again?"

"No. How would I?"

She shrugs. "He seems like a resourceful man."

I narrow my eyes. "Speaking of being resourceful, have you thought about my dilemma?"

"Changing the topic?" Abigail says with a slight eye roll. "Fine, here's what you do with the cash sitting and doing nothing in a bank: invest forty percent into index funds, then twenty percent—"

What follows is much more boring than the earlier turtle/tortoise treatise, and it includes dreaded math, but I force myself to listen and ask what I hope passes for intelligent questions.

When Abigail is finished, I ask, "Do you think I can afford to have some fun?"

She grins. "You can afford to have so much fun it might just kill you."

"Then I'm taking a Royal Ruskovian cruise," I announce.

Ever since a frenemy in middle school went and then told me all about it in excruciating detail, I've been wanting to go.

"You can afford to rent a private ship," Abigail says.

"No, I want that whole experience. I want them to seat me at a dinner table with some random people from Iowa. I want a huge crowd at the nightly magic show. I want—"

"Norovirus? The flu? Covid?"

"I'll just wash my hands," I say determinedly. "I take it you don't want to join?"

She shakes her head. "I already have plans for the break."

I open my mouth to ask her what said plans are, but someone clears their throat.

A masculine throat.

I turn toward the sound and nearly choke on my sushi roll.

It's him.

The Viking.

Mason Tugev.

The hockey player billionaire whose looks I've been doing my best to forget, but now that said looks are in my face, I can't help but stare at their fierce beauty.

And then it hits me.

I'm at school.

He's not a student.

Frowning, I demand, "What the hell are you doing here?"

Chapter 8

Mason

An hour earlier

"I'll take whatever your easiest course is," I tell the confused child working in the bursar office. "Introductory Astronomy, Music Appreciation, or Intro to Russian. I'm not picky."

After some back and forth, I find myself enrolled in "Introduction to Physical Education"—a course that I could probably teach much better than the professor. The reason for my sudden interest in adult education is simple: the security at the university is pretty tight, so this is the easiest way to get a valid student ID and access to all the buildings.

Once inside the campus, I head over to the cafeteria, and as I go, I can't help but wonder how Max found out what time Sophia and her friend have lunch every day. Sophia doesn't seem to be on social media, so unless he learned it from the friend's feed, he must've accessed the school's cameras or something like that.

As I approach Ladybug, I see that she's in the middle of a conversation with a blonde friend of hers.

Fuck me. Said friend is wearing something that might as well be a gross Halloween costume: a shirt with giant pink buttons.

I take a soothing breath. I'm here. I might as well get this over with.

Feeling a modicum less grossed out, I open my mouth to clear my throat, but before I get the chance, Ladybug says, "Then I'm taking a Royal Ruskovian cruise."

What the fuck? Why? Theodore owned a yacht, which is now hers.

"You can afford to rent a private ship," the blonde replies.

Or use a better cruise line, or—

"No, I want that whole experience," Ladybug says. "I want them to seat me at a dinner table with some random people from Iowa. I want a huge crowd at the nightly magic show. I want—"

"Norovirus?" the blonde counters. "The flu? Covid?"

Not to mention filthy idiots hitting on her non-stop, an idea I passionately dislike.

I have no time to clear my throat before Sophia replies, "I'll just wash my hands. I take it you don't want to join?"

The blonde shakes her head. "I already have plans for the break."

Before Ladybug can continue this inane conversation, I finally clear my fucking throat.

Wait. Was that rude? Ladybug turns, frowning at me the way the principal would back in school whenever I'd put a puck through a gymnasium window.

"What the hell are you doing here?" she exclaims.

I take a deep breath. "Hi. I'm sorry I interrupted you." There, I can be cordial... if I *really* try.

"Hold up." The blonde's eyes, glinting impishly, dart from me to Ladybug and back. "You're Mason, right?"

"Don't talk to him," Ladybug hisses at her friend before turning to glare at me. "He was just leaving."

"Yes, I am Mason," I reply to the blonde. "And you are?"

"Abigail," the blonde says. "I'm Sophia's best friend, so she's told me all about you."

"She has?" And was it an angry rant?

"If you don't leave, then I will." Ladybug leaps to her feet.

Seems like the time for niceties is over. "You said you'd consider selling me the team."

She purses her lips. "And I have." Standing straighter, she announces, "I am *not* selling."

"Don't you want to know how much I'm offering?" My hands ball into fists before I can stop them, and Sophia notices. In fact, she stares at each one with a strange—likely terrified—expression.

I unclench my fists. The last thing I want any woman to fear from me is violence. I consider men who hurt women the lowest lifeforms on the planet. In fact, they are lucky that I'm not in charge of running this world because they would cease to exist in that scenario.

"I don't care about the price," Sophia says. "I'm not selling." She doesn't add, "to you," but I'm pretty sure that's what she means.

"That's stupid," I snap before I can think better of it.

"Ah, yes," she says, words dripping with venom. "Calling me stupid makes me so eager to do business with you."

"I didn't call *you* stupid." If anyone is stupid, it's me for saying that word in front of a woman. "I was calling the strategy of not-selling-the-team-without-knowing-how-much-you-could-get stupid. What if my price was twenty times what the team is worth? Thirty? Fifty?"

"Maybe you both should take a calming breath," Abigail suggests. "You might want to discuss all this… over dinner."

A dinner where Ladybug poisons my food?

"You stay out of this," Ladybug says curtly to her friend.

Abigail raises her hands. "Fine."

I take a calming breath as per her earlier suggestion. "Look, Sophia, if you're not selling, what do you plan to do with the team?"

"That's none of your business," Ladybug growls. Unlike me, she seems to have done whatever the opposite of taking a calming breath is.

My teeth clench of their own accord. "I'm on the fucking team. That makes it very much my business."

She sits back down. "I will think about what to do. You're not going to be consulted. Bye."

"You don't know anything about sports, or running a team," I grit out. "Or business in general."

Her nostrils flare. "I'll learn. I'm sure if a caveman like you thinks he can do it, I'll have no trouble at all."

"That's a good burn... a rarity for you," Abigail whispers to Sophia approvingly. She gives me a challenging look. "I can help her with the business side of things, in any case. So no need for you to worry your handsome big head over it."

And on that note, the two of them return to their conversation, which for some reason now involves cramps and tampons. In case they decide to discuss buttons next, I take this as my cue to leave.

They may have won this period—and I mean in the hockey sense—but I will win the match.

Chapter 9

Sophia

"**A**nd for an extra heavy flow," I say, keeping a poker face. "You know, the type that's like a scene from *Texas Chainsaw Massacre*, I use Tampax Pearl—"

Abigail chuckles. "He's gone."

"Finally." I grin like an evil villain. "Typical man."

Rupert, my ex-whom-I-do-my-best-not-to-think-about, would gag at any hint of "that time of the month," even if it was something innocuous, like a discussion of punctuation marks or a trip to Tampa.

"To Mason's credit, he lasted longer than I would have expected." Abigail waggles her eyebrows. "Speaking of, you should also check his stamina... in bed."

"What?"

She rolls her eyes as she snatches the last piece of sushi with her chopsticks. "You should let him take you out—to discuss business, of course, and afterward, invite him over for some... Netflix."

"We don't own a TV."

"Exactly," she says. "Though given the vibes between the two of you, maybe you should be less coy and invite him over for a hate fuck."

Yeah, no. I'm not the type who can invite someone over just like that, but even if I were, that someone would *not* be that man. Thanks in large part to Rupert, I want nothing to do with men, be it a relationship, hate fucking, or even asking them to screw in a lightbulb.

"I can see you're overthinking this," Abigail says with a sigh.

I counter with a sigh of my own. "Can we talk about something else? For example, how is your job search going? Did you apply at Octothorpe?"

The anxious expression on Abigail's face makes me regret asking. "I applied but didn't hear back from them. I do, however, have a few interviews with other companies lined up after finals. What about you?"

"No jobs on the horizon," I say. "But as it turns out, I don't need the money so urgently anymore."

I feel a pang of guilt as soon as the words leave my mouth. It's almost like my father had to die in time for me not to worry about replacing Abigail as my roommate. Shit. Speaking of. "Want to have a sleepover at my new mansion?"

Abigail jumps excitedly to her feet. "I thought you'd never ask."

As Richard gives us a ride, Abigail tells me what she's learned about managing a hockey team.

Turns out, the cost of the team includes the arena, the players, and the staff.

"I own an arena?"

She nods. "Yeah. In Brooklyn. You also own Mason... in a way."

"How does any of this make money?" I ask, ignoring the bit about Mason.

"Ticket and merchandise sales, sponsorships and TV contracts," Abigail says. "There may be more that I haven't yet delved into."

The sushi in my stomach becomes cold and clammy fish once again. "I already feel overwhelmed with my newfound wealth. This team sounds like a major extra headache."

"You don't know the half of it," she says. "You'll need to increase revenues and/or cut costs. The media outlets and fans will have a lot of questions for you. The—"

"Maybe I *should* sell?" I wonder out loud. "Not to that asshole, but to someone?"

"Whatever you want to do," Abigail says. "Like I told him, I can help you figure all of this out."

I open my mouth to reply but notice the awestruck expression on my friend's face.

Ah.

Right.

We've arrived at my not-so-humble abode.

"Yeah." I take it all in once again. "It's big."

She grins. "That's what you'll say to Mason one of these days."

Before I can come up with a retort, Effie leaps out of the entrance and bows like a proper butler.

Abigail's eyes gleam as she takes in all the ink adorning Effie's skin.

"Abigail, this is Effie, the butler," I say.

"Do you have a brother?" Abigail blurts.

Seriously? Even if she does, it's not like tattoos are genetic.

"I'm an only child," Effie says, her expression confused. "Why?"

Because my friend wants to have sex with your non-existent sibling—and maybe with you too, at least a little.

"No reason," Abigail says, blushing. "You just seemed like the type."

The type to have a brother? Is it a certain deadness in the eyes that a sister develops after enduring countless stupid pranks?

"Would you like another tour?" Effie asks, changing the subject.

Nice save. "Yes, please," I say. "I'm not familiar enough with the place to do it justice."

This is how I get another walkthrough and Abigail gets her first. A few times I have to elbow my friend because whenever she spots a representation of turtles, she giggles maniacally, which makes her sound like Floki from *Vikings*.

"Ready to see the gardens?" Effie asks.

Abigail nods.

We head over to Donatello and April's domain and find them doing exactly the same thing they were doing the last time I was here: humping like rabbits, though I think I might henceforth change that expression to "humping like tortoises."

"Wow," Abigail whispers. "That's a big bang."

I grin at her.

"Don't stop," we suddenly hear Acadia scream at Donatello. The doctor clearly hasn't noticed us approaching or doesn't care if she's overheard. "Keep going. Just like that. Yes. Yes. Yes!"

Effie and I exchange confused glances while Abigail whispers, "Rule 34."

I believe Rule 34 states something along the lines of "whatever it is, it's someone's porn," and if so, my friend is right. The good doctor may just have a little fetish for big reptiles doing it, but who am I to kink-shame when I get wet at the sight of a fist?

"Want to see the garage?" I whisper to Abigail.

She nods and we head over there, where Abigail chuckles at the sight of the turtle-like Beetle.

"What's next?" I ask Effie.

The butler shrugs. "You tell me. You've seen the whole house now."

I scratch my head. "What about something like a kitchen?"

Effie shuffles from foot to foot. "You saw the dining room."

I frown. "Right, but where do I go when I get hungry?"

"Well, duh," Abigail says. "You go to the dining room and tell your amazing butler what you want."

Given the grateful look Effie shoots at my friend, I bet if there were a tattoo-covered butler brother, she'd offer him as thanks.

I turn to Effie. "I don't get to raid the fridge?"

Effie wrinkles her nose, clanking her jewelry in the process. "Just tell me what you'd hypothetically be looking for, and I'll get it."

"What if it's the middle of the night?" Not that I've decided if I'll sleep here on a regular basis, but I will tonight.

"She does get hungry for sweets at the weirdest times," Abigail whispers to Effie conspiratorially. "It wakes me up every time she opens the stupid fridge."

"You can still call for me," Effie says, but she looks less sure now.

"I wouldn't feel right doing that," I say.

"Therefore, she'll go hungry," Abigail chimes in. "Which means she'll be cranky the next time you see her."

Effie seems horrified at the idea of a cranky "mistress." "The kitchen is this way, but please only use it in case of emergencies."

So we visit the kitchen and explain to the cook—an older lady we met earlier—that she's not going to be redundant and that I'm only going to show my face in this room when craving a doughnut at night.

"Okay," the cook says. "What kind of doughnuts are your favorite?"

I tell her, and she promises to make a couple to keep in the fridge at night.

Wow. Whoever says money can't buy happiness clearly hasn't considered homemade doughnuts as a variable.

"Can you make us some dinner?" I ask the cook. "With popcorn as an appetizer?"

When Abigail looks at me questioningly, I explain that I want to watch a movie with her in the "media room" and then have dinner.

"Yes!" Abigail pumps her fist. "This is going to be the best slumber party ever."

———

"So," I say to Abigail the next morning as Richard drives us back to our micro-apartment. "Do you want to move into my mansion with me?"

She furrows her perfect brows. "Commuting to school will take forever."

I gesture at Richard. "But we'll do it in style."

Abigail puts a hand on her belly. "I'll gain four hundred pounds."

She's got a point. Last night's dinner and today's breakfast were fancy-restaurant quality but fast-food quantity. And I won't even count the midnight doughnut I had, one that I still think might've been a wet dream.

"There's a gym," I remind her. "We can work off the meals."

She cocks her head. "If I say no, will you leave me on my own?"

"No. But I'd want to rent us a better apartment."

She shakes her head. "I can't afford to pay half of anything better. Not unless I get a job."

"That's fine," I say.

"No, it's not." She tucks a strand of blonde hair behind her ear. "Crashing in your mansion would be one thing, but an apartment is a whole different story. I can't let you—"

"Yes, you can. You're helping me with this team business for free, or did you forget?"

"How about we have a few more sleepovers at the mansion?" she says in a tone that tells me her mind is set in stone. "Then we'll talk."

Translation: after said sleepovers, she will tell me what's what—which is fine.

"Do you have a parking spot?" Richard asks, and I realize we're pulling up to our street.

"A parking spot?" Abigail grins. "Sure, it's next to the stables."

"Can you drop us off and look for a paid parking garage?" I suggest.

Parking here will cost an arm and a leg, but I need to start thinking like a wealthy person.

Richard nods, but because there's a big truck sitting by the building's entrance, he lets us out down the block.

As we head down the street, I notice a man walking a strange spotted dog, and something about the man's broad back seems familiar.

"Hey," Abigail says, following my gaze. "Isn't that—"

Yep. The stranger turns, and it's Mason, in all his virile glory.

"Are you stalking me?" I demand, advancing on him.

Mason raises an eyebrow. "I'm just walking my cat."

I pause my glare to check out the strange dog I saw earlier, who, in fact, does turn out to be a large cat. An adorable cat, with pointy ears and leopard-like coloring.

I narrow my eyes at Mason. "How did you know I like cats?"

Because I do, and I've always dreamed about getting one, except it's never been possible. Before our landlord's rules got in the way, it was my mom's cat allergy, not to mention her inability to keep even the single human in her care, i.e. me, properly nourished.

Mason's dark eyebrow arches higher. "How could I know that you like cats?"

"The same way you know where I live," I snap, motioning to my building. "And where I go to school."

Mason squeezes his hand over his cat's leash, a

gesture that makes his hand look too much like a fist for my panties' comfort. "Spike and I have been together for four years. I just met you. I'm not that good of a planner."

"What kind of a cat is he?" Abigail croons, staring down at Spike.

"A Savannah," Mason says proudly. "Before you ask, he's a rescue, and I know the city doesn't allow his breed, which is why I have a special license for him."

"He's super cute," she says.

"It's true," I say grudgingly. I have no idea how much said license cost or how it was even obtained, but a woman with giant turtles who fuck nonstop shouldn't throw stones.

"Thank you." For the first time since our meeting, Mason smiles, and I wish he wouldn't, because it makes his already attractive face too much so, to the point where it affects my lady bits in the same way that a premium fist would.

I do my best to shake it off. Sternly, I say, "Seriously, what are you doing here?"

"I came to apologize." His hand dives into his tracksuit pocket. "And to give the two of you these." He hands me two papers.

"Tickets?" Abigail exclaims. "Are they for—"

"End-of-season," he says. "Center ice, right by the glass."

They must be good seats because Abigail's eyes widen to comic proportions. Just as I open my mouth to reject the shady offer, she starts jumping up and down like a teen about to go to her favorite boyband concert.

"Thank you! Thank you! Thank you!" she gushes. "I was dying to go!"

I glare at Mason, who gives me a look that says, "Are you really going to take this away from your best friend?"

"Okay." I snatch the tickets from Mason's hand—a big mistake because my fingers brush his, and it's like all the electric power of Thor's mighty hammer zips through my body. "Thanks," I grumble as I jerk my hand away.

Mason looks wonderingly at his fingers that were just holding the tickets. "No... problem."

"Well, then," I mutter. "We have somewhere to be."

"Have coffee with me." He makes this sound like a foregone conclusion.

Shit. Am I really tempted?

As if sensing my weakness, Spike rubs himself against my leg, purring like an overactive vibrator.

Wow. Has he trained his cat to wear me down?

Maybe not just the cat. At my side, Abigail's nodding so fast that she looks like a human bobblehead.

"I'm sorry, but no," I say more to Spike and Abigail than to Mason.

And before feline cuteness is further weaponized, I sprint for our building's entrance.

———

It's not until we're both safely inside the apartment that I realize something that should've occurred to me earlier: I own the team and the stadium, so I don't need tickets to go to the game. In the same way that I don't need an invitation to come to my own party.

Grr. To think that for a second, I felt grateful to the man.

"So why not have coffee with him?" Abigail demands as I'm still processing that he somehow pulled a fast one on me.

I grit my teeth. "Because he's a jerk, and it was just an excuse to talk to me about buying the team." As I speak, I turn on the most luxurious item in our place: the tiny cappuccino maker.

Abigail watches me with exasperation. "Look at what you're doing. You're even craving coffee. You totally should've said yes."

If craving something were a reason to agree, I'd have two. "I just need caffeine for my lecture on Platonic idealism."

Abigail snorts. "I don't care how much you plan to lecture me; I will not agree that keeping things platonic with a man like Mason is ideal."

Unsure if she's kidding or not, I can't help but explain, "According to Plato—"

"Your right boob or the ancient Greek dude?" she interrupts.

I sigh. It was a mistake to tell her the secret nicknames for my breasts: Plato (on the right) and Socrates (on the Left). I named them thus because my mammary assets are big, and in philosophy, it doesn't get any bigger than Plato and Socrates.

"I meant Plato the Greek," I grumble. "He believed that the physical world is not as real as ideas—or forms—are."

"The dude must've been on something," Abigail says. "Or watched *The Matrix* one too many times."

I know this comment is to bait me into geeking out about all the philosophy in *The Matrix*, so I ignore it. "Things in the real world are mere imitations of the ideal forms. So, for example..." I gesture at the micro-microwave. "Somewhere—don't ask me where—exists the Platonic ideal for a microwave, and ours is a lousy imitation of that ideal."

"Which can be said of a microwave inside the Matrix," Abigail says triumphantly.

I shrug. "Maybe that's what I'll learn in the lecture, but I'll never know unless I'm awake. There's a reason everyone calls our professor Ambien."

Finally, she leaves the issue of coffee with Mason alone, and we have breakfast and caffeinate before I rush to my lecture.

———

I'm sitting in front of an ice rink, eyes bulging at the sight of the players: all naked as mole rats, but much, much hotter.

Then I spot Mason, and he's hotter than all his comrades combined, and that's before I notice his tight fist clenching his hockey stick and his other fist stroking his hard cock.

Everyone around me cheers, as if jointly urging Mason to come.

Meeting my eyes, Mason gives himself an expert stroke and adroitly sends the puck into the opposing team's goal.

Not sure which stick he used for that, but it turns me on unbearably.

Though I've never thought of myself as an exhibitionist, I ignore all the people around me as my hand sneaks into my panties and my finger circles my clit. Once. Twice.

"Sophia!" Mason screams as his strokes intensify. "I'm coming for you, Sophia. Sophia!"

"Sophia?" the voice of Professor Ambien is like a cattle prod poking me in the butt.

Fuck me. Despite the precautionary cappuccino, I've still managed to doze off and drool all over my desk.

"Care to tell us in what text the Theory of the Forms was first introduced?" Ambien asks nastily.

I rub my crusty eyes. "*Phaedo?*"

Ambien looks disappointed. "You should thank Zeus for your habit of studying ahead. Class participation is twenty percent of your final grade, and you almost lost it."

Shouldn't he invoke Morpheus as his Greek god of choice, seeing how that's the dream deity and all?

"In any case," Ambien drones on, "In *The Republic*, Plato—"

My eyes become heavy again immediately, so I bite my tongue to stay awake.

The last thing I want is to return to that dream where I saw Mason naked.

Chapter 10

Sophia

"These tickets are amazing," Abigail exclaims when we take our seats on the day of the game.

My cheeks burn. Being here reminds me too much of the recurring wet dreams I've been having for the past two weeks, but there's no way I'm telling Abigail— or anyone else—about them. Unless… maybe I should tell a therapist? I guess I can afford one now, and unpacking my traumatic childhood does sound like a fun way to spend my time.

"Look." Abigail points at the ice. "Number Forty-Two."

I can't help but look, and there Mason is, wearing a hockey jersey that doesn't make him look bulky, the way it does other players. Instead, the uniform teases me with the promise of him taking it off.

Wait, what? He won't take it off. Not unless I'm dreaming again.

Hmm. Am I dreaming? The players aren't naked,

but the agility and skill they display on the ice is mind boggling, especially in Mason's case.

Example: he skates forward, leaving his teammates behind, and then trips over the hockey stick a guy from the opposing team—Number Thirty—put in his way. If that were me, I'd wake up in the hospital with a concussion, but Mason merely drops to one knee (as if proposing) before shooting the puck from that position. And... he scores!

"Did you see that?" Abigail shouts. "He got it right between the goalie's legs!"

Ignoring my friend, I start watching in earnest, and I'm spellbound when Mason scores another goal.

"That was incredible," says a nearby fan to another. "He stayed with the puck, pirouetted, went between the d, and then scored between the legs."

Yeah. It was pretty incredible, and I'm beginning to see that scoring is something Mason is very good at—as well as getting between people's legs.

The game keeps going, but then Number Thirty smashes into Mason right next to us.

Hey! Is that even fucking legal? Mason might be an asshole, but I don't enjoy seeing him bashed like that... or seeing anyone bashed, really.

Thankfully, Mason is okay, or so I assume, since instead of falling down in pain, he throws a punch right at Number Thirty's face, and the crowd erupts in response.

I gasp, my hand flying to my mouth. All I can think of at first is that I saw a glimpse of a real fist. Then I'm petrified because Number Thirty punches Mason back.

Or tries to. With a grace of a figure-skating tiger, Mason dodges said punch and then lands another hit, right in the fucker's eye. Everyone around us goes wild, with an explosion of cheers for Mason and obscenities for his opponent.

Wait. Why am I angry at Number Thirty all of a sudden? Why do I want to see him in pain? Is this what drove the Vikings—this kind of bloodthirst?

I blame groupthink. The fans clearly want Mason to win.

The stripey-clothed referees arrive on the scene, and I fully expect them to eject Mason and/or Number Thirty from the game, or at least give them a harsh penalty.

Nope. I clearly underestimated the levels of violence considered acceptable in hockey. The refs do nothing to either man and allow them to return to the game as if the recent blows were merely an exchange of salty words.

"Dude," Abigail says, fanning herself. "If you don't sleep with him, someone else might."

She may have a point. To our right, a group of blondes are drooling and ovulating, their vulturous gazes on Mason.

Grr. Now I can relate not only to a regular Viking, but to a berserker as well. Something green is making me want to howl like a wild animal, foam at the mouth, and collect blonde scalps.

Wait, that last one might not be something the Vikings did.

Further stoking my ire, Mason looks in the direction of the blondes—or so I think at first.

Abigail elbows me in the kidney, proving that violence begets violence. "He's looking for you."

It's unbelievable, but it's true. Mason locks eyes with me and winks.

Winks!

Before I can even process the butterfly effect happening in my belly, a teammate passes Mason the puck.

Whoosh. Mason turns into a human torpedo, careening toward the goalie, sliding into the midst of enemy defense like a well-lubed cock into a—

"Goal!" that same overeager fan screams nearby, just as the crowd goes wild again.

Okay. It's official. If all hockey is like this, I just might like it, even if it goes against my pacifist nature.

A bit like Vikings.

The game continues in the same vein, with Mason a rockstar throughout.

By the end, the Yetis win, and the stadium roars in celebration.

"Do you want to go to the locker room?" Abigail shouts into my ear over the racket. "Talk to the team?"

I shake my head vehemently. "They might ask me questions like, 'What are your plans?' Not to mention, Mason will try to pressure me to sell again."

Abigail sighs with resignation. "Can we at least get a drink?"

I nod, and we exit the stadium in search of a bar.

"Bailey's cookies and cream milkshake, again?" Abigail asks disapprovingly as the bartender sets the mouthwatering concoction in front of me.

I shrug. "It's the closest thing this bar has to dessert."

She rolls her eyes. "It *is* dessert."

In answer, I take a nice big sip of my drink/dessert and force myself not to wince—the bartender was heavy handed with the alcohol.

"So," Abigail says after she gulps her low-carb beer or whatever she got. "Did you book the cruise yet?"

I nod. "It's in a week. Right after finals."

She frowns. "Aren't you moving into the mansion around that time?"

I feel a pang of guilt at the reminder. After some deliberation, I decided to live in the mansion, but Abigail insisted on staying in the apartment we've shared all this time. It took a lot of arguing, but I was at least able to convince her to let me pre-pay my part of the rent for the remainder of our lease.

"Richard said he'd take care of the move," I say. "I'll just put my stuff into boxes after I pack for the cruise."

Abigail pouts. "I'll miss having you around."

"Same. But look on the bright side... You'll get to

sleep on the bottom bunk, or—and this would be an insane luxury, I know—get a normal, one-person bed."

Of course, she could just get another roommate for the bunk bed, but that idea makes me weirdly jealous, which is silly considering that I have the choice of staying in the tiny apartment with Abigail... at least until she finds a job, which probably won't take that long.

"Wait a second," she says, interrupting my thoughts. "Isn't that...?"

I follow her gaze and nearly choke on my dessert—I mean, alcoholic beverage.

Mason has just entered the bar, along with a crowd of dudes whose faces I recognize from the game.

This is the whole Yetis team, no doubt here to celebrate their win—and they're not alone.

The blondes I saw earlier are with them, and though it shouldn't matter at all, for some reason this makes me angrier than a Tasmanian devil whose juicy carrion has just been stolen.

Setting down my drink with a bang, I leap to my feet and head right for Mason.

Chapter 11

Mason

A s soon as we walk into the bar, my eyes zero in on Ladybug, and my fucking cock gets harder than a hockey puck—and those things can break the bones in your hand.

I blame the dress she is wearing. It's low cut and shows off her perfect breasts in all their ivory glory. It doesn't help that I've always been a boob aficionado, even if said boobs are attached to someone I shouldn't want anything to do with.

Fuck me. It's bad enough I thought about this woman each time I jerked off in the past two weeks. Now she's giving me hard-ons while being dressed? If my teammates didn't love this bar as much as they do, I'd punch a hole in the wall, but after the last such incident, the owner said he'd ban us if we broke so much as someone's nail.

I check if my teammates are staring at Sophia, ready to break bones instead of walls if they are.

Nope. They're too busy with the horde of blonde puck bunnies that accosted us outside.

I grit my teeth and blame my intense swirl of emotions on the endorphin rush from the win. My teammates and I did all we could to burn off the crazy victory-related energy, from butting heads (a celebratory tradition in our sport) to hugging it out. This trip to the bar was supposed to be a continuation of the jubilee, but now it's ruined, at least for me.

No. Wait. Maybe I can ply her with drinks and ask her to sell?

Or maybe not.

As soon as Ladybug spots me, her eyes narrow into tiny amber slits.

Pretty slits, but still.

She strides angrily my way.

This is not good.

"Don't follow me," I bark at my boisterous teammates and hurry forward to meet her out of their earshot.

To my surprise, not a single nosy busybody comes after me—probably because they're too occupied with the blondes.

Ladybug and I come face to face in about the middle of the bar, and she nearly crashes into me, her ample bosom heaving and driving my cock insane.

"Are you stalking me again?" she demands.

I curl my upper lip. "Yeah. I always bring my whole team when on the prowl."

"Don't you mean *my* team?" Even her nostrils flare in a pretty fashion, somehow.

With an effort of will that should win me some sort of peace prize, I raise my hands, palms out. "I swear on our next game, I had no idea you'd be here." She looks slightly mollified, so I go on. "Why don't you let me buy you a drink? I promise not to pester you about selling the team."

It will be one of the hardest things I've ever done, second only to not staring at her breasts, but if I manage to bury the hatchet with her once and for all, then maybe when—

"Fine," she says, much to my shock. "One drink."

"Two." I have no idea why I just said that. The more drinks, the more chances to make a social faux pas— one that will likely involve her boobs.

"It's a deal."

She leads me over to her friend—Abigail, I think her name was. The friend's expression reminds me of the one Spike gets when he corners a hapless spider in the corner to "play with it."

"I've just realized I have to head out," Abigail says and feigns regret very poorly.

"Why?" Sophia demands.

"It's related to my job search," Abigail says. "A friend of a friend told me they know someone at Octothorpe. I want to talk to them ASAP."

Emergency job search conversation? At night? She couldn't come up with something better?

To my surprise, Sophia seems to buy it because she says, "Can you at least stay for one more drink?"

"Sure," Abigail says.

I motion to the bartender. "Another of whatever the ladies were having and a vodka for me." Turning back to Abigail, I say, "You know, I have a good friend who works at Octothorpe. If tonight's connection doesn't work out for you, I can make an introduction." And considering that tonight's connection is imaginary, why would it work out?

"That would be amazing." Abigail's eyes gleam excitedly, confirming the suspected lie.

For the first time, Sophia looks at me with almost no hostility. "Why would you do that?"

I shrug. "If Abigail were to get the job, Landon—that's my friend—would get a generous recruitment bonus from Octothorpe and therefore owe me one."

"Ah, of course," Sophia says and picks up a giant white glass from the bar. "I should've known that it would somehow benefit you."

I gape at the monstrosity in her hands. "What is that?"

Abigail chuckles, and Sophia gives her a stare usually reserved for me. "It's a Bailey's cookies and cream milkshake."

I squint at the atrocity in the glass—which dwarfs everything around it, even Sophia's ample bosom. "Are those crushed Oreos?"

"Yes," Sophia says with an eyeroll. "The drink has the word 'cookies' in the title."

"And fudge?" Though I'm not into sugary concoctions, an image pops into my brain, one where I'm smearing fudge over her pale, smooth, perky—

"It's used as a topping," Sophia says. "It's delicious."

I surreptitiously rearrange my cock. "It probably has a quarter of my daily calorie intake."

Wait. I shouldn't have said that. I blame too much blood being away from my brain.

The slitty eyes are back. "Are you calling me fat?" Sophia hisses.

Abigail steps back, like she's worried her friend might explode.

"Your body is actually perfect," I say earnestly, and my cock strains against my boxers, as if in confirmation.

A blush spreads from her face down to her breasts, and it makes me want to toss her over my shoulder, caveman-style.

"Doesn't vodka have a ton of calories?" Sophia gestures at my drink.

"Touché," I reply. "A single shot is about a hundred calories, which is why I only indulge on a rare occasion." And I don't want to develop an addiction like my grandfather—the one who supposedly died of alcohol poisoning before I was born.

Good. Thinking about my family has slightly dampened my libido... that is, until Sophia takes another breath, causing her breasts to rise and fall.

Abigail sets her empty glass on the bar with a thud.

"I hate to interrupt all this diet-oriented flirting, but I really have to go."

"Good luck," Sophia says.

"Thanks," Abigail says and rushes away.

Sophia turns back to me and takes a big sip of her so-called drink. "Do you think there was a job thing, or was she just trying to leave us alone?"

So she's not as gullible as I thought. "The latter, I'm sure."

She cocks her head—and even that gesture is sensual when she does it, which is insane. "Could you *really* help her get a job at Octothorpe?"

"Of course." I take out my iPhone. "Let's exchange our contact information so you can pass me her resume."

"How very Machiavellian." She pulls out her phone. "You just want my number."

I shrug.

She downs the rest of her dessert, then texts me and makes sure I text her back.

"Let me get you another drink." I warily eye her empty glass. "Do you want the same thing?" I hope she says no because if she stomachs another one of those things, she might become diabetic and go into a coma on my watch.

She examines the bottles behind the bar. "Want to do tequila shots with me?"

I wince. "Tequila doesn't agree with me." In that the alcohol tolerance afforded to me by my Estonian genes goes out the window when I drink tequila—and this is after accounting for the fact that most brands of tequila have higher alcohol by volume content than most vodkas.

Sophia's sexy evil grin makes me regret my admission. "It's either tequila or another milkshake. Your choice."

I wave at the bartender. "Two shots of your best tequila."

"I can't believe it," Jason says, arriving with Parker just as the shots hit the bar. His speech is slurred. "You said you'd never drink 'worm piss' again."

Fuck. I forgot the team was here, and now these two bozos have snuck up on us.

"Jason, Parker, this is Sophia," I say pointedly. "The new team owner."

"Oh," Jason says stupidly.

"We're going to be leaving," Parker says, sounding much soberer than Jason, though that's a low bar.

"Before you go." Sophia downs her shot like it's water. "It's not a worm that you see inside bottles of mezcal. It's moth larva."

Why doesn't mention of worms or moth larva help my stupid erection subside? Did one of my children—I mean, teammates—slip me some Viagra?

Jason elbows Parker. "Even the women he likes sound like nature shows."

I glare at them both. Parker quickly gets the picture and drags Jason away to the dance floor, where they immediately start grinding on the blondes.

"Is Jason on the team?" Sophia asks. "I don't remember seeing him on the ice."

"He's the goalie, so his mug is thankfully covered by a mask during games, sparing our fans the horror."

"Is that a joke?" Sophia cocks her head again. "His face is actually quite handsome."

It won't be after I punch said stupid face, even if I have no idea why I suddenly want to. "You want an introduction?" After he sobers up, of course, and checks out of the hospital I'll put him in.

She shakes her head. "I don't date brutish men. Or even find them attractive." She doesn't add "present company included," but I can tell she wants to.

I grit my teeth and take the shot, then grimace.

Whether we're talking worm or moth larva, it's still insect piss.

Sophia seems to enjoy my expression. "Another shot?"

"Is this a challenge?"

She replies by ordering four more tequila shots, "the cheaper the better."

Fuck me. I've never tried the cheap stuff, but I've heard it tastes even worse, as hard as that is to believe.

"Cheers," Sophia says and throws back the first shot, her face gleeful instead of grossed out.

How bad can it be?

I take the shot and gag. It's like someone extracted the needles from the fucking cactus this drink was made from, dipped them into sewage, and scraped them down my throat.

And yet, miraculously, I'm still turned on.

"Another?" Sophia asks with a hiccup.

I glare at her. "Bring it on."

What am I doing? She's twenty-four and has the excuse of her frontal lobes still developing. I'm over a decade older and supposedly wiser, so I should put an end to this... but I take the shot glass, close my eyes, and experience the horrific taste once more.

"Admit defeat?" She gestures at two more shots.

Does she not understand what it means to be a *competitive* athlete? I drink not just the shot designated for me, but hers as well—and surprisingly, the last one doesn't seem as bad as the rest.

"Give up," I say when I catch my breath. "You'll get alcohol poisoning way before I do."

"Yeah, no." She orders four more shots, uses two to catch up with me, then nods at the next one. "Want to give up?"

"No, but if that's what it takes to save you from getting your stomach pumped tonight, so be it." I push the tequila away.

She bats her fluffy eyelashes at me. "You care about my wellbeing that much?"

"No," I lie. "I just figure that if you were to kick the bucket, whoever would inherit the team after you might be an even bigger pain in the ass."

"Ah," she says over a hiccup. "I'm the devil you know?"

"Exactly," I reply, then realize I'm talking to her boobs instead of her face, so I lift my gaze.

"Sounds more like a bunch of excuses." She grins devilishly—which hopefully means she didn't notice where I was looking. "Lightweight."

I'm the adult—or so I remind myself, over and over. "How about we pause our drinking contest for a few minutes and have a dance-off instead?" I suggest.

Given how much she's had to drink, she'll have enough trouble getting up from that chair, let alone managing a dance move.

To my shock, she gets to her feet with only a slight wobble, though even that might be my slightly blurred vision playing tricks.

Hmm. Maybe the last few drinks haven't hit her liver yet?

I get up from the barstool myself, and the world around me slides around a little, as if I were back on the ice but without my skates.

Noticing my discomfort, Sophia arches an eyebrow. "Ready for that dance-off?"

Ready or not, I extend my hand to her, and when she takes it, the feeling of her soft skin on my callused palm makes my already-hard-for-too-long dick scream Estonian obscenities.

When Sophia isn't looking, I readjust myself so I can walk despite the monster hard-on.

Somehow, we get to the dance floor.

My teammates make a wide circle for us, but their partners—the blondes—seem unhappy about something, at least if I go by the dirty looks that they give Sophia.

Sophia leans in and her juicy lips brush my ear, turning my cock green with jealousy and balls blue with—

"Instead of competing," she whispers, "do you want to do a more cooperative sort of dance?"

I draw back to stare at her dumbly. "Why?"

"Because I'll concede the tequila contest if you say yes," she says.

"No, I mean why dance 'cooperatively?'" And doesn't that merely mean "dance together?"

She shrugs. "I feel like making your little blonde fan club jealous."

"Fuck, yes." Wait, did I say that out loud? Well, whatever. I pull her so close that I can taste her mango-and-watermelon scent. "Let's fucking dance."

Chapter 12

Sophia

The dance floor spins, but Mason keeps me anchored—or, more precisely, his crotch does as I grind on it with my backside, twerking-style. Actually, if we're being precise, it's his *hard cock* that is my anchor—at least I assume that's what's jutting against my ass, and not, say, his hockey stick.

My plan to make the blondes jealous might be going a little too well. All of them look ready to eviscerate me, then fry up my innards and enjoy them with a glass of my blood.

Also, I'm afraid the blondes were just an excuse. The sad truth is, I wanted to dance with Mason.

No. That's tequila talking.

Mason isn't—

A slow song begins to play, and strong arms turn me around.

"Need a break?" Mason asks, his voice husky.

I shake my head, not trusting myself to open my

mouth because if I do, that hard cock of his might end up in there somehow.

He takes my hand and places his other hand on the small of my back before we start to sway to the music, as if it were prom night.

Kill me now. Mason smells how I've always imagined a Viking would: equal parts birch, ice, and testosterone. His nearness makes Plato and Socrates's nipples as hard as the cock that's now against my belly.

"Do you think they're sufficiently jealous?" Mason murmurs into my ear, words slurred.

"Who?" Plato and Socrates? They *are* kind of jealous of my lower back and hand, where Mason is touching me.

Mason smirks. "Did you forget why we're dancing 'cooperatively?'"

I furrow my brow. Oh. Shit. He's talking about the blondes. In my state of hyperarousal, I completely forgot they existed—but the feeling isn't mutual as they are still darting hate-filled glances my way.

"I didn't forget," I lie. "But now that you mention it, there's something else we can do that would really make them jelly." I moisten my dry lips and give him my best come-hither glance from under my eyelashes.

A wildness sparks in his eyes, and it is as frightening as it is exciting.

His voice is a low growl. "I think I know what you're talking about." He dips his head.

Without meaning to, I lean toward him, lifting on tiptoes.

His lips crash into mine, and he swallows my gasp.

Mason kisses just as fiercely as he plays on the ice, and I love every millisecond of it. It is so good, in fact, that the bar and the rest of the world become a distant memory. All I can feel is his rough lips, his exploring tongue, and his ever-growing hardness against the softness of my belly.

Oh, and did he just cup Socrates? I think he did, and I love it, just as I love his other hand on my ass, pulling me closer and closer and—

The world comes back into view in the form of the Yeti team cheering and hooting at us like a pack of syphilitic owls.

Mason grudgingly pulls away from me and growls something murderous at his teammates.

The bar spins around me, and I clutch at him to stabilize myself. "Do you want to get out of here?" I mutter when he returns his attention to me.

Eyes gleaming feverishly, he grabs my hand, and we rush outside—as though the blondes might be chasing us with glued-on nails filed into claws and garrotes made of hair extensions.

I blink dazedly at the blurry, streetlight-illuminated street. "Where to—" I hiccup. "Where to now?"

He gestures across the street. "My place?"

"You live inside the stadium?" Is that even legal? Also, don't I own the place and therefore—

"No." He takes my chin and turns my head slightly to the right, his touch making my body break into goosebumps. "That building, right next to it."

If some part of me wasn't sure if going over to his place was a good idea, that last touch seals my fate.

"Let's go." I grab his hand, and I guess I pass out from the resulting zing of lust because the next thing I'm aware of is riding in an elevator, our tongues dancing like Wednesday's hands to Lady Gaga's "Bloody Mary." Or to whatever the original song in the show was.

The elevator dings open into an apartment, and we're stripping our clothes as we half-kiss, half-walk through a very long corridor. Then something—hopefully Spike, the cat—hisses at us.

"Sorry," Mason breathes, pulling away momentarily. "I think I stepped on his tail."

I have no idea why, but what comes out of my mouth in reply is, "The only pussy you should be concerned with is mine."

My words clearly strike a chord. Mason growls like a berserker, lifts me off my feet, carries me into his bedroom, and lays me down like a sacrifice on Odin's altar.

My suffocating dress is promptly removed, as is my bra, leaving Socrates and Plato free, their nipples almost painfully pebbled.

"Gorgeous," Mason rumbles before he rips my panties off like they were made of tissue paper.

Did I mention he forms a fist in the process? Well, he does, and this is officially the wettest I've ever been in my life.

Panting, I watch him strip his own clothes, all the way down to his boxers.

"Those too." I gesture at the tented underwear with a trembling finger.

He removes his boxers, unleashing the cock that I've been feeling against me all night.

Wow. Just wow. It's big, thick, velvety, and otherwise so perfect that it might just be the Platonic ideal of a cock, one that makes all other cocks seem like limp imitations in comparison. I can't help but think of Nietzsche and his Übermensch. Also, to slightly paraphrase Nietzsche, if you gaze long enough at this cock, the cock will get inside you.

Yep, I hereby christen this cock Uber.

"I want it in me," I blurt.

Mason's nostrils flare. "Not until I taste that pussy."

"Oh. Well. I guess I can be patient."

With a smirk, he bends down and gives my pussy a featherlight kiss.

My whole body turns into a shiver.

Mason's callused hands cover Plato and Socrates, and his strong fingers tweak their nipples with just the right amount of pressure—like he's had years to learn what I like.

His next kiss lands on my clit, and it's firmer and more wonderful than his last.

I lean back and close my eyes, overwhelmed by all the sensations.

He laps at my folds, making me moan in pleasure. Then he places another kiss there. And another. Then he licks and circles my clit with his tongue before kissing it once again.

My moaning grows frantic and desperate as the pressure starts to coil in my core.

He releases Plato and Socrates—and they miss his touch immediately. But then his palms slide under my butt cheeks, and he pulls me toward him, his tongue penetrating me as if to give a prelude of what Uber will do.

Just as the orgasm is almost upon me, he places his tongue on my clit, making it flat and pliant—and then he pulls my ass toward him once more, and I come with a scream.

"Good girl," he murmurs roughly. "Now come all over my fingers."

One of his hands releases my butt, and he slides one finger inside me, then another, all while his lips and tongue take their turns at my oversensitive clit.

The feeling is intense, and the orgasm only takes a few seconds to fully form and crash into me, hard. I come even louder this time, and by the time I catch my breath, he's arranged me on all fours, ass and pussy exposed from behind for his viewing pleasure.

His voice is a low, deep growl. "So. Fucking. Hot." He rips opens a condom and sheaths Uber. "Are you ready for me?"

"Hells yeah," I gasp. "But... can you do something for me?"

"Anything." As if to confirm the words, Uber twitches.

"Can you grab a fistful of my hair?" I undo my ponytail. "And then hold it so that I can see it?" I've always wanted a guy to do that as he fucks me, but I've never felt bold enough to ask.

His jaw ticks. "As I said, fucking hot." Gripping my hips, he enters me, shallowly at first, then pushing deeper and deeper until I'm deliciously stretched—and then he reaches forward, grabs a handful of my hair, and holds it in a tight, veiny, white-knuckled fist within eyeshot.

Fuck! I shouldn't have asked him for that. The surge of arousal is so extreme my vision speckles with white. There's something animalistic about how much I want him to fuck me. Something desperate.

"Faster," I pant, staring at the fist unblinkingly. "Harder. Please!"

With a grunt of pleasure, Mason speeds up his pace, pistoning into me with the same breakneck speed as when he skated toward the enemy goal.

My entire body feels like a pulsing wave of sensations. "Mason! Oh, fuck, Mason..."

He takes my words as an invitation to go faster and harder, his free hand squeezing my ass as his other continues to grip my hair in that glorious fist.

"Come for me," he growls, slamming into me with powerful thrusts, pushing me over the edge.

With a gasping cry, I come, quivering around him.

"Fuck," he grunts, and I feel him harden before he grinds against me in his own release, giving me a final aftershock of pleasure that leaves me completely worn out.

"That's it," I gasp as he pulls out of me. I plop on the bed. "I'm going to pass out now."

"Sure thing, Ladybug," he murmurs, wrapping his hot body (in every sense) around me. "Sweet dreams."

Ladybug? Whatever. After the pleasure he's given me, I'd let him get away with calling me a scorpion. Maybe even a cockroach or a dung beetle.

Closing my eyes contentedly, I keep my word and pass out.

Chapter 13

Mason

I wake up to an excruciating headache. It's sharper than the time I got hit with a puck that was traveling a hundred miles per hour. It also has a more nauseating pain texture than the time I got bashed on the head with a hockey stick.

Maybe someone slammed my head against the ice this time? Or maybe they're doing it right now?

No. The foul taste of tequila on my breath brings back some of the events from last night.

Sophia challenged me to a drinking competition.

Wait. Sophia.

I blink open my eyes and ignore the hellish pounding in my temples. She's here, wrapped all over me, like the most wonderful blanket in the history of blankets.

Oh, shit. It's all coming back to me now, including the part where I fucked her... and how amazing that was.

Or did I dream that part?

I gently slide her off me and sneak a peek under the covers.

Yep. We definitely fucked for real. I must've passed out before it occurred to me to discard the condom because there it is, still on the bed.

I grab the condom and carefully slide out from under the covers. As soon as my bare feet touch the floor, I stagger into the bathroom and use half a bottle of mouthwash in an attempt to rid myself of the tequila taste.

It doesn't help. Neither does brushing my teeth. Giving up, I shuffle over to the kitchen and chug my custom-made electrolyte drink, which consists of coconut water, green tea, and freshly squeezed kale juice.

The drink seems to help a bit. Now instead of feeling like I'm being murdered, I merely feel like I'm being tortured.

Then it hits me. I've just drunk the whole concoction. When Sophia wakes up, she'll need electrolytes as much as I did, or maybe even more.

So, despite the headache, I force myself to make more of the drink. I even add some carrot juice for sweetness—Ladybug seems to have a sweet tooth.

Drink made, I decide to also fix us some breakfast. Eating helps when hungover, even if it's often the last thing you want to do.

As I chop the veggies, I let myself process the disaster that was last night.

I slept with my team's owner.

No. Worse.

I got her drunk *and then* slept with her—and the fact that I was drunk myself is not a good excuse. The woman loathes me when she's sober, so she only slept with me because of the tequila. Worse yet, I wanted her before the drinking even began. I blame her big boobs. And that mischievous glint in her amber eyes. Not to mention—

There's a loud thud in the bedroom.

Fuck! She must have fallen.

I sprint over there for all I'm worth, cursing myself for leaving her alone in the first place.

To my huge relief, it's not Ladybug's body that's on the floor. Instead, my mattress is.

"Sophia?" I look around, then check under the bed.

It's like she's vanished into thin air.

Then I hear water running in the bathroom.

Rushing over there, I knock.

No reply.

"Sophia, are you okay?" I loudly demand.

"I'm peachy," she shouts over the sounds of running water. "The mattress just slipped."

Yeah, right. She must still be drunk.

I wait for her to finish, pacing the hallway as I do.

As I approach the bookshelf, one of the trophies I have displayed at the top tumbles toward my head.

Thanks to my hockey-honed reflexes, I catch the thing and glare up.

As expected, it's the cat.

"That's not funny," I growl.

He looks like he disagrees. I sigh. No matter how many times I chastise him for such pranks, he still seems to think that pushing shit onto my head is fun. And so is dropping insects he kills into my food.

Spike's retort is a look that seems to say, "I could've woken you up in the middle of the night again, but I was merciful."

Then again, maybe he did try to wake me. I was so drunk I wouldn't have noticed.

"Do that again, and there will be no salmon for a month," I threaten, putting on my best poker face to make sure he can't tell that I'm bluffing. Not giving him salmon is like not letting me on the ice—a form of cruel and unusual punishment that I obviously would only do for a day or two.

Spike swishes his tail, leaps down from the bookshelf, and rubs against my leg.

Yeah. That's better. Too bad the threat only works for a very short while.

Done sucking up, Spike walks over to one corner of the room, where he takes great pleasure in shredding a lacy piece of fabric with his claws.

Wait a fucking second. "Bad cat," I say to him sternly. "Those were Sophia's panties."

Speaking of Sophia, the water in the bathroom has stopped. I sprint back and wait for her to open the door—which feels like it takes another ten hours.

Finally, the door swings open, letting out a bunch of steam. Ignoring it, I scan Sophia for signs of injury. I find none, thankfully. To my disappointment, she's completely dressed. And to my envy, she doesn't look nearly as hungover as I feel.

"Are you stalking me by the bathroom now?" she asks curtly.

"What?" My headache intensifies as though the trophy did smash into my head.

"Forget it." She takes in a deep breath, and her breasts bob up and down, making my cock stir. "I'd better go."

"Wait." I gesture in the direction of the fallen mattress. "Are you positive that you're okay?"

Also, I recall she's not wearing any panties, and the stirring in my cock turns into a monster hard-on.

She narrows her eyes. "Of course, I'm not *okay*. I never should've slept with you, that's for starters. I also shouldn't have let you convince me to drink all that tequila."

I stagger back. "I convinced you?"

"Whatever." She passes by me so closely I can smell the familiar notes of mango and watermelon. "I'm leaving now. Don't you dare follow me."

And before I can so much as offer another rebuttal —or the electrolyte drink—she rushes out of my apartment.

I exchange a confused glance with Spike, whose gaze seems to say, "May I suggest getting yourself neutered? It might make your life a lot easier."

Chapter 14

Sophia

A few minutes earlier

I wake up with a jolt, feeling as sick as a dog who was poisoned by an evil cat.

Where the hell am I? Why do I feel so hungover and yet also drunk?

As soon I look around and spot my scattered clothing everywhere, it all comes back to me in a rush: the bar, Mason's fist grabbing a handful of my hair, and —relatedly—all the orgasms.

Speaking of… where is Mason? Did he leave me by myself in his place? That would be pretty odd.

Then again, I should be glad he's not here. Things would be infinitely more awkward if he were.

Maybe I should take advantage of his absence and get myself the hell out of here?

Yes, I should.

Determination and adrenaline clear my brain

enough to allow me to get up from the bed. All right. I locate and put on my bra, ignoring the hickey on the side of Socrates.

Where are my panties? I search high and low but don't find them. Fine, whatever. I put on everything else before I return to the mystery of the missing panties. I look around more thoroughly, but still, I can't find them anywhere.

Maybe I should leave them behind? No, that's weird. Then he'll have a memento of the night I would rather us both forget. Besides, I'm feeling a little too vulnerable without them.

I look around again.

What the hell happened to them? Did Mason eat them last night? There is such a thing as edible panties, and we were pretty drunk.

No.

I think I'd remember him acting like a freaking goat.

I strain my brain and call forth a vague recollection of him ripping the panties off me at one point. Unfortunately, all that does is make me feel as though they'd melt anyway if I had them on right now.

I scour the room once more. Even if the panties were damaged by Mason's rough treatment, they should be here somewhere, right? The guy is strong, but he's not strong enough to break panties into atoms and scatter them in the air.

I kneel and look for them under the bed.

Nope.

I move the nightstand away from the wall and look behind it.

Zero panties.

Could they somehow have gotten under the mattress? Things did get pretty wild, so it's theoretically possible. Heaving with effort, I lift the mattress as much as I can, but all that accomplishes is the mattress sliding from the bed and hitting the floor with a deafening thud.

Fuck me. If Mason hasn't left the apartment, he'll be here in a second, and I'm not ready to face him—or explain why I was checking under the mattress like a thief from back in the day when the banking system did not yet exist.

Grabbing my shoes, I beeline for the bathroom and make myself presentable as I ponder how I ended up making such a monumental mistake.

I blame the alcohol, obviously, and his competitiveness... and mine. What I try not to think about is how much I enjoyed what happened because that was also just the alcohol, right? With enough tequila, even a scarecrow might start to look fuckable, much less the sex-on-a-hockey-stick that is this man.

Midway through my bathroom activities, there's a knock on the door.

Fuck me.

The voice is deep, sexy, and unwelcome. "Sophia, are you okay?"

"I'm peachy," I shout back. "The mattress just slipped."

What are the chances he accepts that and leaves?

Apparently zero, because when I finish and stealthily open the door, there he is, looking so mouthwateringly hot that I'm tempted to go for round two.

Wait, am I insane?

"Are you stalking me by the bathroom now?" I snap, as angry at myself as I am at him.

"What?" he asks, frowning, then winces.

I should be glad he's also suffering, but the opposite is the case. "Forget it." I take a breath to clear my head. "I'd better go." Before I somehow end up in his bed again, or on that mattress on the floor. Or on the carpet. Or the bare floor.

The temptation is shockingly strong.

"Wait." He gestures toward said mattress. "Are you positive you're okay?"

Is he mocking me? "Of course, I'm not *okay*," I grit out. "I never should've slept with you, that's for starters." Understatement of the century. "I also shouldn't have let you convince me to drink all that tequila."

He does a double take. "I convinced you?"

"Whatever." If I'm honest, maybe I played a bigger role in the tequila debacle than I'm willing to admit—and worse yet, maybe I used that as an excuse to end up in the exact situation we're in. "I'm leaving now. Don't you dare follow me."

There. I stomp out, but a part of me—granted, that

same insane part that wants more orgasms—hopes he doesn't listen and chases me down.

But he doesn't.

Which is good.

Right?

When I'm outside, I take out my phone and see a million texts from Richard.

Shit. Yet another blunder: after he gave us a ride to the stadium, I let Richard wait for us, then got drunk and forgot all about him.

I scan the messages guiltily. They start off being merely politely inquisitive, then slowly become more and more panicky.

I call him right away and spend a good fifteen minutes reassuring him that I'm not dead in a ditch somewhere, and that I could use a ride.

"I'll be there in a minute," he says, still sounding relieved that I'm not dead.

"A minute?" I ask.

"Yeah," he says. "I'm still near the stadium."

I'm the worst. "Did you sleep in the car?"

"Yeah, but it's not a problem," he says. "Just tell me that you are okay next time."

Next time? There are walks of shame, but it seems I'll have a ride of shame. "I'm so sorry," I say earnestly.

"I'm just glad you're okay," he says again and hangs up.

There will not be a next time. If there's any chance I might go out and get drunk, I'll take an Uber.

Wait.

I *did* ride something I dubbed Uber last night.

A blush spreads over my whole body at the memory.

How mesmerized was I by Mason's cock that I forgot that the word Uber is already in use?

Well, I'll use Lyft from now on, or Richard. I doubt I can "ride an Uber" ever again. Not without getting wet.

Then something else occurs to me. It just might be Richard's fault that I called Uber "Uber." Richard wants everyone to call him Dick, and he's my ride service, so maybe, subconsciously, I've begun to associate dicks with car rides?

As it so often happens when I think about the subconscious, the philosopher in me starts to ponder questions such as, "Can you prove that people besides you are conscious?" An even more interesting one is: "Are animals conscious?" If they are, what about flatworms? Some flatworms tear themselves in half when they want to reproduce, and then those halves regrow the lost body parts to become two flatworms, with apparently intact memories. What happens to flatworm consciousness during such a process? If it's retained, it means body parts can have a consciousness, and if that is the case, it makes me wonder if Plato, Socrates, and Uber are conscious.

A car honk distracts me from my philosophical musings, so I reluctantly climb into Richard's car and spend the ride home apologizing.

————

"Tell me exactly what happened," Abigail demands during lunch on campus the next day. "Don't skip a single detail."

Yeah. Sure. That last bit isn't happening, but I do give her a PG version of the events, glossing over how much I enjoyed myself. Despite my censorship, Abigail listens with a worrying expression on her face, like either her brain is about to explode or she might have an orgasm vicariously.

"So what's next for the two of you?" she demands when I finish.

"Nothing." No selling him the team and no Uber rides for me.

She waves away my words like she would an annoying fly. "Has he called you?"

"He has." And I've ignored his incessant calls, as well as the texts, and even one email—and that last one was weird because I don't think I gave him my email address.

Abigail's face sags. "You didn't answer him, did you?"

"And I won't. Don't even try to talk me into it."

She looks at something over my shoulder, and her grin reminds me of what Spike might look like if he ate a canary. "What about talking to him face to face?"

I follow her gaze.

Fuck.

Headed our way is Mason, and he is holding a lunch tray with his big hands looking too much like fists for my comfort.

"I've just remembered I have to edit a paper." I leap to my feet and rush out of the cafeteria as if I were the aforementioned canary and Mason were Spike.

I'm so overwhelmed by the near-miss that I'm wide awake in Professor Ambien's class, which is bad. Ambien sucks so much as a teacher he almost makes me dislike philosophy. In that, the lecture reminds me of the scene from *A Clockwork Orange* where the anti-hero's eyes were clamped open for aversion therapy.

As Richard drives me home after class, I check my phone and find a few more messages from Mason, my favorite one being:

Running away? How very mature.

He's got a point. I should face him and calmly explain that I don't want to see him, but I can't bring myself to do that, and not just because saying that would be a bald-faced lie. I think a part of me is afraid I'll end up having another orgasm.

"You should eat your dinner," Richard says, meeting my gaze in the rearview mirror.

Ah. Right. There's a lunch box next to me, and when I open it, I find the chef's latest masterpiece: crepes with Nutella and berries, with bits of egg, ham, and cheese.

As I eat it, I realize I'm quickly getting adjusted to my newfound wealth—and not just gastronomically. Over the past two weeks, I've gotten to know the staff and figured out an efficient way to run my household. Thanks to Abigail, I have a firm grasp on some of my investments—the exception being the hockey team, but even that seems to be running itself for the time being.

As we pull up to my mansion's gate, I spot a person loitering nearby. I recognize her immediately, and the temptation to pretend I'm not in this car is very strong.

"Who is that?" Richard asks.

I sigh. "My mother."

Chapter 15

Sophia

Richard pulls over, and I don't stop him, though I should.

Instead, I get out and look her over, my heart squeezing painfully.

Mother looks so terrible that her "before" and "after" photos could be used for an anti-drug campaign.

"*Agápi mou*," she says, making my heart squeeze even harder.

"Hello, Eleni," I say.

She chuckles bitterly. "No more 'Mama,' huh?"

"How did you find me?" She's one of the two reasons I don't do social media, the other one being Rupert.

When she frowns, I realize most of her wrinkles are frown-specific, and almost none show that a smile has ever touched her features.

"How did I find you?" She snorts. "You make it

sound like you didn't want to be found by your own mother."

Where do I even start? "I know about Dad. I know he didn't actually abandon me. That you made up that whole thing."

She narrows her eyes at me, and just as with the frown, you can tell this is something she's done often enough to leave permanent grooves in her face. "I'm 'Eleni' and he's 'Dad' all of a sudden? That *malákas* was a domineering control freak, and I'm happy he's dead!"

I blow out a frustrated breath. I mean, what did I expect she would say? Still, I feel compelled to try. "Controlling? Is that because he asked you to check into rehab?"

She flattens her lips. "He also told me what to wear and how to speak."

Translation: he probably asked her not to dress like a street walker and curse like a sailor on Odysseus's ship.

I sigh, deeply. "Why are you here?"

"I wanted to see you."

I spin in place. "There. You saw me. Bye."

She bristles. "Aren't you going to invite me into your new mansion?"

"I can't," I say gently. "You know that. I can't be your enabler any longer."

Her chin quivers in a perfect imitation of Claire Danes. "So you'll leave me to starve on the street?"

"Eleni… Mom…" I drag in a breath. "How about another rehab? I'll pay for it. Just choose the best one.

It'll be like staying at a resort—all your needs taken care of."

She lets loose every Greek curse I've ever heard and some I haven't, culminating in a very English "ungrateful bitch."

It takes everything I have to maintain my cool. "That is my best and final offer," I say evenly when she's finished. "When you're ready to accept it, let me know."

And with that, I get back into the car and tell Richard to get me home, fighting tears the entire time.

———

Even as far back as six hundred years BC, the Ancient Greeks noticed that the moods of patients improved whenever there were horses around. This is how the concept of pet therapy started, but I doubt anyone has used giant tortoises in such a capacity before me. Unless Dad did? Either way, today is a rare day where I don't catch Donatello, April, and Dr. Kelpcon mid-coitus, and I find that watching them graze on the grass —just the tortoises, not Dr. Kelpcon—is extremely soothing, which is exactly what I need after the encounter with my mother.

Eventually, I'm calm enough to study for my upcoming finals and even finish a couple of papers.

When my studies are complete, I reward myself by playing a video game on the giant screen of my private movie theater. The game in question is *Assassin's Creed Valhalla*. In it, I play a Viking who unapologetically raids towns, kills hordes of people, and slowly expands her influence over Ancient Britain.

You know, exactly the kind of game a pacifist like me should be playing.

I'm just meeting Ivarr (one of the more bloodthirsty sons of Ragnar) for the first time when Effie walks in with my dinner, bowing in that way that must've been drilled into her at the Hogwarts School of Butlery.

"Ah," she says. "You're about to look for King Burgred."

"Hey, no spoilers," I say sternly, then grab the food and get absorbed in the game again until I'm so tired that I start to fall asleep mid-battle. At that point, I head to my very luxurious and very tellingly not-a-bunk-bed.

Except now that I'm here, sleep eludes me. As usual, thoughts of Mason are the cause. Or if I'm being honest, horniness keeps me up.

Grr. I hoped that after all that gaming, I'd finally go to sleep without resorting to masturbation, but that is not to be.

Grabbing my vibrator, I go to town down south, doing my best not to think of Mason's fist... and, unsurprisingly, failing.

Chapter 16

Mason

"Come on, Suit, one more rep," Jason urges. Landon grunts as he benches twice his body weight.

It won't be good for his already-overgrown ego for me to tell him so, but that is pretty impressive. Doubly so when you remember that unlike my teammates, Landon isn't a professional athlete and doesn't need to be in top shape for his white-collar job.

"Does he play?" Parker whispers into my ear as Landon does yet another rep, veins popping on his neck.

I shake my head. Another thing I won't be telling Landon is that Parker's question is a huge compliment: it's the equivalent of saying "this dude looks hockey-player tough."

"So, Mason," Landon says when he's off the bench. "Do you own the team yet?"

I ignore the question because he knows perfectly

well that I don't. He's just trying to get a rise out of me, which makes me want to hit him upside his fucking head with a dumbbell. "Are you at least working on it?" Jason asks worriedly.

Does sleeping with Sophia count as "working on it?" What about all of my pathetic attempts to communicate with her, the ones that I'm not even sure were about team acquisition?

"I have a plan." I give Landon a glare that says, "I could choke you with that barbell, and everyone would think that I merely failed to spot you in time."

My sinister glare clearly fails because Landon says, "If by 'plan,' you mean 'the most stalkerish stunt I've ever heard.'"

The ears of all my nearby teammates perk up, and Jason speaks for them all when he asks, "What's the plan?"

I glower at them.

Landon says, "I was sworn to secrecy."

"Secrecy means not even hinting at whatever the secret is," I grit out to Landon before turning to Jason. "It's need to know, and you don't need to know."

My teammates are big gossips, and I don't want Sophia to somehow catch wind of my plans since that would ruin everything.

"Fine, next topic," Jason says as he grabs some dumbbells and lies on the bench to do flies. "What's everyone doing for the holidays?"

They all take turns sharing, but I stay out of the conversation. Every year, I pretend to spend time with my family because I can't bring myself to tell Landon or my teammates the truth: my parents do not want to see me or even hear from me, especially during the holidays, and even more so if the holidays are religious in nature.

It's fine, though. Spike is like family to me, and we can have a nice Christmas by ourselves.

———————

Muscles pleasantly sore from the workout, I walk on my desk treadmill and review my investments. As is my new usual, thoughts of Sophia distract me, but somehow, I refocus and buy a few stocks that Landon suggested earlier. Since it was Landon's suggestion that led me to buy Octothorpe at the right time, I treat his investment tips with a lot of respect.

After I'm done with stocks, I attempt to contact Sophia again.

Nope.

At this point, I don't expect a reply, but I guess I'm still hopeful, though that hope is fading fast. It's looking more and more likely that I'll have to resort to what Landon has dubbed my most stalkerish stunt.

In fact, yes, I've decided.

If Sophia doesn't miraculously reply to my last message by the time I finish walking Spike, I'll pull the trigger on my plan.

There is a big problem with walking your cat, and it's called dogs. In Spike's case, this is extra tricky because he's more of a danger to many of the dogs we meet than vice versa. He could badly hurt even the fiercest breeds if they forced his claws—though such dogs would have to go over my dead body first. Interestingly enough, Spike likes dogs and has a few friends among them—ones who didn't behave like jerks upon meeting him when he was a kitten.

This is why he looks excited when he spots one such friend—a papillon named Sir Francis.

"Hello," says Jack, one of the people who usually walks Sir Francis.

"Hey," I reply.

This is the downside of friendly dogs; you have to socialize with their handlers. But hey, listening to Jack drone on and on is worth it because Spike seems to be having a grand time—and even takes it in stride when Sir Francis sniffs his butt and tries to hump him.

I guess that's the ultimate dog compliment? If so, then Spike returns it when he licks Sir Francis's giant fluffy ears.

I don't know why, but watching this idyllic play makes me think about starting a family one day, a human one, but also maybe with a friendly-to-Spike dog. The weirdest part is, Sophia's face—and boobs—come to mind at this exact moment. But that's insane.

Speaking of insane, when Spike and I get home, there is no reply from Sophia.

Am I doing this then?

To make sure the decision isn't driven purely by my dick, I jerk off—thinking of Sophia as I do.

Once my mind is clear again, I reanalyze my options. Nope, still don't see any alternatives. With an outward sigh—and more than a little inner excitement —I get onto my computer again and put my plans in motion.

Okay, it's done—and I feel the same way I do when I execute a daring play on the ice.

Sophia doesn't realize this yet, but like many goalies, she's about to find me pretty difficult to ignore.

Chapter 17

Sophia

"To winter break!" I raise my cafeteria-made Fanta-knockoff in a toast and look around.

Abigail pouts. "I still have another final to take."

"Sucks to be you." I playfully stick my tongue out at her while still keeping an eye on my surroundings. You never know when a rogue hockey player might show up. "This is my last chance to salute you before I depart for Port Canaveral. Richard is waiting for me outside to take me to the airport, and then once I'm on the ship, I will be incommunicado."

She sighs. "You know you can afford to get Wi-Fi onboard, right?"

I scoff. "I don't care how rich I am, I'm not paying those prices for Wi-Fi, especially when it's so much slower than what I have at home. In any case, no internet is part of the charm. A digital detox. I'm even leaving my phone in airplane mode for the duration."

"Airplane mode?" She looks aghast.

I shrug and then sneak a look around once more. "Vikings sailed without social media, and they loved it."

"Are you planning on a lot of killing and pillaging?" she asks.

"Just shopping and sunbathing when we're on land, and looking meditatively at the horizon while we're at sea."

"Sunbathing in the winter?" She wrinkles her nose.

"Beats trudging in snow." This time, I look behind me, just in case.

When I turn back around, Abigail is looking smug. "Are you hoping that he'll show up?"

"No." Maybe. It's stupid, I know, but I want to get a glimpse of him before I depart. Unfortunately—I mean, fortunately—he stopped stalking me physically a couple of weeks ago. Even his texts and calls have ceased in recent days.

"You could just call him back," she suggests.

"And encourage him to resume the stalking?"

She rolls her eyes. "It's not stalking if he genuinely goes to this school. I know the girl in the bursar office who got him registered."

Questions like, "What girl?" and "Is she pretty?" are on my lips, but I don't want to give Abigail any ammunition.

Abigail's face turns serious. "Why are you so against giving him a chance? Everyone thinks you're together, anyway."

She's talking about a disreputable tabloid that took pictures of me and Mason as we left the bar on F-Day.

If they are to be believed, Mason and I are minutes away from tattooing each other's names on our genitals.

"He doesn't want a chance with me, if that's what you mean," I say. "He wants his precious team, and I'm just a means to that end."

And hey, at least he's open about needing something from me—unlike Rupert, who fucked me literally on the way to fucking me figuratively.

"It didn't look like he wanted the team the other day," she says. "It looked like he wanted *you*."

I shake my head. "You're wrong, but it doesn't matter. Even if I decided to start dating someone, it wouldn't be a guy like Mason." A guy I could see myself falling for all too easily—a surefire way to get my heart shredded yet again.

"Who said anything about dating?" She waggles her eyebrows. "A lot of fun can be had without such drastic measures."

"Yeah, no." The more orgasms I have, the closer I shift to the point of no return, and Mason has already given me as many as Rupert did in our first month of dating.

Abigail sighs. "Maybe you'll meet someone on the cruise?"

"Maybe." But I highly doubt it.

From here, we chat about nothing of substance until the food is gone, at which point I text Richard to let him know I'm ready to hit the road.

As I walk through campus to the car, I catch myself

still looking around for Mason—with no luck. But just as my ride comes into view, I feel a hand land on my shoulder. A masculine hand.

Feeling oddly elated, I turn, expecting to see Mason's chiseled, Viking-like face... only to lay my eyes on its complete opposite.

"Hi, baby," Rupert says, his smile as fake as the Rolex knockoff on his bony wrist. "Long time, no see."

Chapter 18

Sophia

No matter how intently I stare at my ex, I can't figure out how I ever found him attractive, let alone thought myself in love with him.

"What are you doing here?" I demand, though I have an inkling.

"Why so hostile?" Rupert asks demurely. "I missed you, so I've been walking around this place, hoping I'd bump into you."

"This 'place' that I almost couldn't attend, thanks to you," I grit out.

"What do you mean?" His brown eyes shine with such innocence that a less world-weary woman might actually fall for it—just as I once did.

"The apartment," I remind him. "The down payment I gave you before you disappeared? That ring a bell?"

His scamming me out of that money turned out to be the tip of the iceberg. Among other things, he also defaulted on the lease for the car that I co-signed for, dealing a final death blow to my credit score.

"Please." He waves my words away like an insect, and I wish I were a Viking—because if I were, pacifist or not, I'd break his arm. "I can explain."

"No explanation is necessary. You've got a gambling addiction—maybe a drug one too—and I was an idiot… but I'm not anymore."

His amicable façade slips for a microsecond, and I see what I always should have seen—a nasty piece of shit. "Is this about your hockey player boyfriend? He will cheat on you with one of his million groupies—we both know that."

I take a step back. "What?"

"Just read the tabloids," he says. "It's all there."

Dammit. Of course someone as slimy as he is would take an equally slimy gossip rag at its word. "Who I'm with, and who they're with, is not anyone's business, but especially not yours. Let's cut to the chase. I know you're here because you've sniffed out money, and you're hoping to scam me out of some, but that's not going to happen."

I should've expected this. What Rupert did to me was very similar to what my mother did before him—and since she's been sniffing around, it was only a matter of time before he did the same.

Rupert puts a hand on his heart—or where one *would be* in a normal human being. "You've got to let me explain what really happened. It was all a big misunderstanding. I was just about—"

Someone angrily clears his throat.

For a second, a fantasy plays out in my mind, one where Mason shows up and does to Rupert what he did to Number Thirty during that game, or maybe even performs some sort of Viking-style ritual execution.

Except it's not Mason. It's Richard, though he's almost unrecognizable with such a fierce expression in his eyes.

"Is this guy bothering you?" Richard asks, putting himself between me and Rupert.

Rupert raises his hands conciliatorily. "We were just having a conversation." Then he examines my vertically challenged driver and, more rudely, adds, "Stay out of it."

"I don't think so." Richard opens his jacket. To my huge surprise, there's a humongous handgun in a giant holster. "In two seconds, you will either be leaving or bleeding," Richard says, the way Clint Eastwood would in the role of Ivarr.

Wow. I wish I had my phone out so that I could capture Rupert's expression. Suffice to say, it's the closest a face can come to resembling a pair of shat-on tighty-whities.

Turning on his heel, Rupert sprints away.

I turn to Richard. "You carry a gun?"

"Well, yeah. I'm not just your driver. I'm your bodyguard."

"Since when?"

"Since always," he says. "Why else do you think you pay me as much as you do?"

I thought it was just the going rate for chauffeurs, but this actually makes more sense... if you forget Richard's diminutive stature.

"Were you in the army?" I ask.

"Army Rangers, to be precise," Richard says proudly, then walks over to open the door for me.

Isn't that a Special Forces unit? Rupert was lucky he left with his tail safely tucked between his legs.

As we drive to the airport, I dodge Richard's questions about my ex by shifting the conversation to the rigorous training Richard undertook in the Army Rangers. And it's only partially because I am genuinely interested. The truth is, I'm so ashamed to talk about Rupert that I haven't even told Abigail, my best friend, the whole story of our relationship. I was so naïve and stupid to be duped like that.

Fortunately, Richard is professional enough to drop the topic, and we chat about my plans for the cruise as he helps get my bags over to security.

After an uneventful flight to the Melbourne airport, I get to Port Canaveral using Lyft, for obvious reasons. Exiting my ride, I lay my eyes on the aptly named *Wonder of the Oceans.*

I stand there, gaping at the ship for a minute, awed by the sheer size of her. If I recall my advertising brochure correctly, this ship can carry ten thousand people, has a full-sized basketball court, a giant surfing simulation machine, a "Central Park" that sounds as big as its namesake in the middle of Manhattan, and in case all of that wasn't enough, it has an ice-skating rink.

Great. Now my mood is slightly soured because that last bit reminds me of Mason.

The closer I get to the *Wonder of the Oceans*, though, the more my mood improves—to the point that if I were a Viking, I'd have a shipgasm.

To my surprise, the crowd of passengers isn't as big as I thought it might be. Maybe I'm early? Well, in any case, since I splurged on an ocean-facing suite, I get the VIP boarding treatment that bypasses the hoi polloi.

When I reach my suite, an unladylike giggle escapes my lips.

The place is huge, and the view from the balcony is what I've dreamed about: unending blue ocean.

After taking plentiful pictures, I plop into a nearby chaise and take a few relaxing breaths.

Amazing. I already feel like I'm on a vacation, and we haven't even set sail yet—or fired up the motor, or whatever the cruise ship does to move.

"This is your captain speaking," says a Russian-accented voice from the sky... or an intercom. The voice informs everyone that his name is Ivan Vorobey, and that we will soon be conducting a muster drill... or passing muster, or possibly, eating something with lots of mustard.

After the spiel is over, I don a yellow (or maybe mustard) lifejacket and make my way to my designated location.

Again, there don't seem to be as many people

around as I would expect—which could be a very good thing when it comes to going on shared attractions such as the zipline and the surfing simulator.

The mustard turns out to be a safety briefing. On my way back to my cabin, I enter the elevator, where I smell ice and birch.

My heartbeat spikes. All of a sudden, I'm thinking of gray eyes, broad shoulders, and Uber.

Dammit. Is this what pining for someone feels like? If so, I hate it, especially since it's directed at a person who is so wrong for me.

Escaping the elevator, I do my best to relax, a task facilitated quite well by the balcony with the ocean view. Then I eagerly dress up for my first on-board dinner. Given the fact that I booked a suite, I have access to a VIP restaurant where I can sit at my own table. However, I much prefer the option to be seated with people from all over the world—the quintessential cruise experience.

When I get to the dining room, yummy smells make my stomach rumble.

The polite hostess shows me to my table, which, strangely, is completely empty.

Hmm. There are plenty of people at some of the other tables—especially the ones farther away.

Odd.

Someone clears his throat behind me.

I don't know how, but even from that nondescript sound, I already know whom I will see.

My pulse leaps into the stratosphere as I spin around.

And yep.

There he is.

Mason Tugev pulls out a chair next to me and descends into it like a king onto his throne.

"Hey, Ladybug," he drawls, sex appeal oozing from his every pore. "What's for dinner?"

Chapter 19

Mason

What's for dinner? After all this time apart, I should've said something less moronic. Maybe rehearsed a speech. Instead, I kept imagining the indignant wrath that would be written all over her beautiful face when she realized what I'd done, and in that, I was spot on because the expression is there, only sexier than I anticipated.

"What are you doing here?" she demands when her delicate jaw returns from the floor.

I shrug as nonchalantly as I can. "I needed a vacation, so I booked a cruise."

For a few moments, she seems to be at a loss for words—probably mentally circling through all the angry rebuttals in her repertoire. "But this is *my* cruise," she finally says, and out of all the possible responses, this one makes me feel a pang of guilt.

The woman wanted to get away, and I've kind of ruined it for her. Oh, well. If she'd just talked to me at any point in the last few weeks, this would've been avoided.

I raise an eyebrow while keeping a poker face. "Between the two of us, this is more *my* cruise than yours."

She blinks at me in confusion.

I gesture at the empty seats surrounding our table and others nearby. "To make sure we could have privacy, I got myself a few extra tickets."

Yeah, "a few" is an understatement. I bought so many tickets for this cruise that I probably could've purchased myself a private yacht instead.

"Hold on." Her eyes narrow. "You've booked all these rooms?" She waves around our table.

"Those and a couple of others," I reply, continuing the business of understating.

Again, she seems at a loss for words, but my attention is diverted by our waiter... or more specifically, by a row of giant white pustule-like buttons adorning his uniform.

Fuck me. I was ravenous a second ago, but now my appetite is but a distant memory, similar to how it would be if someone brought the feces of maggots or the deep-fried poo of a dung-beetle to our dinner table.

I frantically scan the room and spot one of the waitresses. Thanks to her dress, I'm spared the horror show that are the buttons.

"Good evening, Mr. Tugev," our waiter says to me. "Good evening, Miss... Papa-Christ-Almighty-birth-doula-Lou."

"Hello," Sophia says, completely unfazed by the butchery of her name.

"We're going to be served by a female member of your staff," I state tersely. "Leave. Now."

The waiter blinks, and Sophia looks on the verge of exploding.

"I assure you I can do as good a job as any of my female colleagues," the hapless waiter says. "Also, sir, you should know that Royal Ruskovian is an equal-opportunity employer that—"

"You can stay if you ditch that." I point at the jacket while trying to avoid looking at the buttons on it.

"I don't understand," he says.

"This is beyond rude," Sophia hisses at me.

Fuck. If she was going to run back to her room before, she's doubly likely to do that now.

I grit my teeth. No choice but to fess up. "I have koumpounophobia."

Sophia and the waiter gape at me with incomprehension.

"A fear of male waiters?" he suggests tentatively.

"Or is it their jackets?" Sophia offers.

"Neither." I gingerly point at one of the vomit-inducing white circles of hell. "Those."

"Buttons?" Sophia asks.

I nod, keeping my gaze away from the damned things.

The waiter looks down at his jacket with a horrified expression. "I can't take it off. I'm not decent underneath."

Sophia meets my gaze, and I could swear that for the first time, we agree on something. Namely, an unspoken question of, "What could he possibly have under there that wouldn't be considered 'decent?'"

"I'm going to switch with Helena," the waiter says before we can delve deeper into the mystery. Running for the matronly-looking waitress nearby, he whispers something to her. There's a lot of pointing at his outfit and at our table.

"Fucking hell," I mutter under my breath. "This is going to be in the tabloids, isn't it?"

"Is it actually true?" Sophia asks, her brow furrowing. "You're afraid of buttons?"

"Not afraid. I merely see them for the disgusting petri dishes of germs that they are." Also, what has possessed me to admit this, of all things?

"Germs?" She cocks her head.

"They've got all those holes for microbes and dust mites to crawl into," I explain.

Sometimes, it's up to four fucking holes.

Way too many holes.

She looks at me as if for the first time. "Did something happen to make you feel this way?"

I force my tense shoulders to unclench. As much as I hate this topic, at least we're talking. "I'm not sure," I say. "My father did once button my dress shirt too tight, and I thought I would suffocate, but I think I was already not a fan of the fucking things and that was just another example of how they can kill you."

Sophia's gaze looks peculiarly soft. Must be those

long, sooty lashes of hers. "That sucks," she murmurs, and I could swear her hand moves toward mine—only in that moment, Helena arrives at our table, smiling as manically as if she were auditioning for the role of the Joker.

"Hello," she chirps in a hoarse voice that hints at two packs of cigarettes a day. "Let me tell you about your menu options tonight."

She slowly recites the menu. When she gets to the sides, she looks at me solemnly. "In your case, I'd recommend skipping the sides altogether, though if you'd like, we can offer you hummus as a substitute."

"Why?" I ask. I mean, I was likely to skip the sides and get something healthier anyway, but how does she know that?

"The options are mashed potato with mushrooms, or pasta," she says, even more solemnly.

"And that's a problem, why?" As she asks this, Sophia's boobs bob up and down most distractingly.

"The pasta is wagon wheels," Helena says, as though that explains anything. "And I'm so sorry about that. The chef didn't know about your situation; otherwise—"

"What are you talking about?" I glance at Sophia in case she has any clue, but she looks as puzzled as I feel.

"Rotelle pasta," Helena clarifies. Seeing our continued blank stares, she blurts, "It kind of looks like buttons."

I clench and unclench my fists, an action that draws a rapt stare from Sophia. "Doesn't that kind of pasta look like *the wheels of a wagon*, which is why people call it *wagon wheels?*" Did someone hire Helena to ruin pasta for me... and wagons?

"My apologies," Helena says. "So you'll be getting the pasta then? It's definitely a better choice than the potatoes, on account of... the young cremini mushrooms."

"What's wrong with them?" Sophia asks, nose wrinkling in more confusion.

"They're also known as button mushrooms," Helena explains.

I exhale an annoyed breath. "Helena, if you're trying to be helpful, please stop. I don't usually eat things like that anyway, but unless your chef is insane enough to deep-fry up some actual buttons, there's no need for you to ruin perfectly fine foods for me by making associations that aren't there."

"I'm sorry," Helena says.

"It's fine," I say. "You said hummus was an option, right?"

Helena nods.

"Do you make it here, on board?"

Another nod, but more uncertain this time.

"I'd like the chickpeas you make the hummus from, just the chickpeas themselves, with five of your side salads without the dressing, and four sides of steamed broccoli—also unadulterated."

As I go on, Sophia's eyebrows turn into question marks.

I answer her unasked question. "I'm an athlete. We

have to watch what we eat." I also eat like this in the hopes of aging slower and more gracefully, but I don't mention that because it will make me sound ancient in the eyes of twenty-four-year-old Sophia.

Helena looks at me pityingly. "I take it you won't be having dessert?"

"Bring me whatever fruit you have in the kitchen," I say. "Berries are particularly welcome." I mention that last part because berries are extra healthy, and in case Helena thinks they look too much like buttons for my liking.

After nodding solemnly, Helena turns to Sophia. "What about you, dear?"

"Oh, I'm not staying," Sophia says, but tellingly, she isn't getting to her feet—which means I might have a chance here.

I turn my best puppy eyes on her. "Please, Ladybug, don't go. I promise not to talk about the team or anything else you don't want to talk about."

Sophia sighs. "Do you realize that you've ruined my chance to meet people from around the world? I was looking forward to that."

"Well, I'm first-generation Estonian," I say. "I can tell you all about the fatherland." And by all about it, I mean the little bit my parents told me, not much of it flattering.

"Fine," Sophia says to me before addressing the waitress. "I'll have the Vidalia onion tart as a starter, the surf and turf for the main course, and dessert."

"Which dessert?" Helena asks.

"Can I try all of them?" Sophia meets my gaze challengingly, but I'm not about to lose my advantage by wincing, even if the temptation is strong.

"Of course," Helena says. "There just might be a small surcharge."

"Put that on my room," I say—even if that makes me an accomplice to the resulting harm to Sophia's health.

"Any drinks?" Helena asks.

"No," Sophia and I say in unison.

"At least no alcohol," I clarify. "I'll have some tomato juice if you've got that."

"And a soda for me," Sophia says, and this time, I must cringe enough for her to notice because she huffs and adds, "Make that an ice cream float."

Does she think she's punishing me instead of her pancreas?

"I'll get right on it," Helena says and hurries away.

"Go ahead." Sophia pouts, bringing my cock's attention to her lips. "Say it."

"Say what?"

"'The food you ordered isn't healthy,'" she says in what she must think is an imitation of my voice. To my ears, it sounds more like that of an ogre.

In response, I shrug. "You're twenty-four. You could probably eat deep-fried chips of lead paint, and your body would survive it... for a while, anyway."

She rolls her eyes. "You sound like you're ninety."

Fuck. She's right, and I was trying to avoid this very thing. "I'm thirty-seven," I admit. "Which means I need to be more careful, especially if I want to play... or not have a heart attack."

Sophia studies me with a peculiar expression. "You don't look thirty-seven."

"Thank you." I raise my water to her.

"Who said it was a compliment?" she grumbles. "I could mean you look like a grandpa, to match the lectures."

Helena comes back with our drinks, sparing me from having to reply.

When we're alone again, Sophia licks the ice cream on her float in a way that makes my already-overzealous cock go into overdrive. "At thirty-seven, aren't you too old for hockey?"

"Showing claws?" I drop a napkin into my lap to hide the bulge, but the napkin tents, so I just move closer to the table.

"Just curious," she says.

"In that case, you have a point. Usually, the retirement age in hockey depends on your position. For goalies, age isn't so relevant, and they actually get better later in their careers. For forwards and defensemen, our performance does tend to decline in our late twenties to early thirties... but I'm fighting against that with all the means at my disposal." And if I live longer as a result, all the better.

"So, when do you think you'll retire?" she asks.

"This is getting too close to the topic I promised to avoid."

"How so?"

I pick up my tomato juice. "The reason I want to own the team is so that they're in my life after I retire."

"Oh." Sophia shifts in her seat. "I—"

"Here's your onion tart." Helena sets the cake-like appetizer in front of Sophia. "And your starter salad." She gives me a plate with two pieces of romaine lettuce and a single cherry tomato.

"What were you saying?" I ask Sophia as soon as we're alone again. I have a feeling that maybe she's started feeling bad about keeping the team from me, especially since we both know it's not a financial decision on her part, but pure spite.

"Nothing," she says, grabbing a piece of her appetizer. "I believe you owe me some interesting facts about Estonia."

I inhale my "salad" in half a bite. "Estonia is the birthplace of the Christmas Tree," I tell her. "Did you know that?"

"It is?"

I smile. "Unless you ask a Latvian. They believe it's their country, but they're wrong."

She grins. "Yeah. Sure. What else?"

I scratch the back of my head. "Taxes are flat in Estonia. That makes filing them so simple you can do it in ten minutes." Or so my parents would lament every time they had to do the same thing here in the States— but I don't mention that part because I don't want her to ask about my family.

"Flat taxes." Sophia fakes a yawn. "How fascinating… if I were an accountant."

I shrug. "It's one of the least religious countries in the world." Which makes the situation with my parents tragically ironic, but there's no way I'll go into that.

"That's a little more interesting," she says teasingly. "Especially if I were running a census."

What would be considered an interesting fact? "Estonia has the cleanest air in the world?"

Sophia shakes her head.

"There are tons of forests that have wolves, lynxes, and brown bears."

"That's a little better. But not much."

"Estonia was the birthplace of Skype," I offer.

She frowns. "Skype didn't originate in Silicon Valley?"

"Nope. It was Estonia—which is also the country with the highest number of good-looking people in the world."

"Is that so?" she says with an eyeroll.

I give her a cocky grin. "I didn't say I was included in that, but yeah, Estonia has the highest ratio of supermodels in the world."

"No, no way." She demands my phone, types something in, and frowns at the result. "Huh," she says, looking up. "Makes me wonder why you aren't dating an Estonian supermodel."

"I don't date," I say, repossessing my phone. "But if I did, it wouldn't be someone from the fatherland, that's for sure." It's what my parents would have wanted if we still spoke, so fuck that.

"I don't date either," she says challengingly.

I'm torn between a weird sense of relief and concern. "Why not?"

"Men can't be trusted," she says with evident sincerity. "Present company very much included."

I cock my head. "I approve of the attitude toward others, but what did I do to you to warrant mistrust?"

"All you want is your team," she says. "I doubt you'd be here otherwise."

I open my mouth to reply, but Helena shows up with our main courses.

After she leaves, Sophia narrows her eyes at me. "What were you about to say?"

What indeed? Maybe I wouldn't be here if it weren't for the team, but maybe I would be. I'm not yet sure about this myself. There's definitely something magnetic about Sophia, and I mean beyond her gorgeous looks and those divine tits. Something about her is—

"I thought so," she says. "But hey, at least you're honest."

I am?

"Are you going to put some dressing on that?" She gestures at my plates—plural.

I examine my food. The appetizer salad had me worried the rest of it would be tiny, but the chef didn't skimp. There are at least two jars' worth of chickpeas here, as well as a couple of pounds of vegetables. "If I were at home, I'd sprinkle some hemp seeds on this," I reply. "But I doubt they have that on the ship."

"Hemp seeds?" She blows out an exasperated

breath. "Of course, you'd consume cannabis but without any of the fun."

She takes a lump of the lobster tail, drowns it in butter, and puts it into her mouth.

Fuck me. The expression on her face is eerily similar to when she comes.

I move my chair even closer to the table and do my best to focus on the conversation. "You are high as we speak, aren't you?"

She shakes her head. "Weed isn't allowed on the cruise."

Since when did that stop anyone? Also… "Why did you check?"

She shrugs. "I don't use it that often, but we're stopping in Jamaica so I was wondering if I could get some there and take it home to celebrate my return with Abigail."

"Ah. So you're the bad influence," I say this with a smile to make sure she doesn't take offense.

"She's a much worse influence on me than I am on her," Sophia says. "I never would have tried alcohol if it weren't for her, or weed for that matter."

"How long have you guys been friends?"

If I had to guess, I'd say many years.

"Since seventh grade." Sophia cuts her steak into small pieces. "She was wearing a skirt, and a bully stole her panties in the locker room. I was wearing jeans, so I gave her mine. She invited me to her house that same day, and the rest is history."

"Wow. That was kind of you—and at an age when kids are pretty much monsters."

"Boys are," she says. "With girls, it's more of a mixed bag."

"You might have a point. I can't picture giving another guy my underwear... or him wearing it for that matter."

She snorts. "I bet he'd wear it if he wore a skirt in an environment with pre-teen boys who like to lift said skirts."

"Maybe. Though he would just as likely give the skirt-lifters a black eye—or a broken nose."

"Like you said." She spears a chunk of her steak. "Kids are monsters."

Am I a monster to her too? I'm a grown up, but if someone tried to lift my skirt—metaphorically speaking —I'd still give them a black eye or even break some bones.

"In any case," Sophia says. "Now that I know weed isn't allowed on the ship, we'll have to celebrate the old-fashioned way—with shots."

I nod. "That's smart. Don't do drugs." It's the one rule that my parents drilled into me that I follow.

She rolls her eyes. "Alcohol is a drug, just a legal one. I saw you partake in *that*."

"Alcohol is a drink," I say. "It's not a drug."

She cocks her head. "You can get high with gummies—and that's food."

"Right, but THC is a drug."

"So is ethanol," she counters.

I cross my arms. "I don't think so."

"It can lead to addiction, right?"

"Sure. But so can cheese—and you don't think that's a drug, do you?"

"Cheese addiction?" She picks up the big shaker of parmesan and sprinkles a good dose on her next piece of steak.

"At least you're not snorting that," I say with a grin.

She rolls her eyes once more. "Alcohol produces endorphins, just like some of the worst drugs."

"Fucking produces endorphins, but that's not a drug, is it?" Then again, maybe that's not the best example. Fucking Sophia might just be the most addictive drug of them all, one that I got hopelessly hooked on from the first try.

Ladybug blushes, then snatches my phone and does a search.

Should I tell her she keeps breaking her digital detox?

"Here." She waves the screen at me. "Alcohol is a central nervous system depressant."

I take the phone from her, read the screen, and frown. "I can tell you're a philosophy major," I grumble in defeat. "You're very good at sophistry."

She looks at me suspiciously, and I belatedly realize that she might not have told me about her major.

As luck would have it, Helena returns at that moment. She's holding a tray of desserts, and helping her is a burly busboy who thankfully isn't wearing the horrible jacket with buttons.

Helena puts a fruit bowl in front of me, then arranges Sophia's desserts around the rest of the rather-large table and hurries away.

I gesture at all the sweets. "Are *those* drugs?"

"No." Sophia gives an éclair a longing glance that makes my cock very jealous. "Well, maybe." She gestures at the tiramisu. "This one has caffeine, which *is* a drug."

I scan the table, amazed at how inventive people can get in their quest to consume as much sugar as possible. "I bet you I could forgo alcohol for longer than you can forgo dessert."

She grabs the phallic-looking éclair. "I'll take that bet... after the cruise."

"Yeah. Sure." I pick up one of the strawberries on my plate. "I don't know if you realize this, but when you crave something sweet, you're really craving fruit." I bite into the strawberry and find it rather sour and therefore unsupportive of the point I'm trying to make.

Sophia sensuously nibbles on the fucking éclair. "Maybe when you crave fruit, what you really want is sugar—and the fruit comes up short."

"Fruit is delicious," I say firmly. "A good ripe mango tastes sweeter than anything you have on this table."

The problem is, fruit needs to be in season, while sugar is by definition saccharine sweet year-round.

"In philosophy, we call this sort of thing qualia," she says. "What the color green looks like to you might be different from what it looks like to me. Same with tastes. Maybe a ripe mango really does taste like a dessert to you, but it sure doesn't to me."

I resist making another comment about her major and dig into my fruit instead. She attacks the desserts, taking a bite of each one but not finishing any.

"Which was your favorite?" I ask when she pushes her chair away from the table.

"The panna cotta." She gestures at a white concoction in a glass. "And I dare you to try it."

I take the proffered tiny spoon and dip it into the fruity part of the concoction.

"That's cheating," she says. "Try the white stuff, without a hint of fruit."

Fine. I fish around for the white stuff in question, all the while wondering what it's made from.

Whatever it is, I doubt it was whole food or plant based.

"Geesh," Sophia says. "It won't bite."

Gritting my teeth, I slip the panna cotta into my mouth.

Hmm. Interesting.

"Thoughts?" Sophia says.

Well, my first impression is that the texture reminds me of the silky smoothness of her pussy, but I've got a feeling that comparison isn't going to be welcome. "It's less sweet than I expected."

"Right, and?"

"A ripe Ataulfo mango has a similar texture," I say. "And if you like this, you'd like leechee nut and cherimoya."

She blows out an exasperated breath. "I give up." She finishes the rest of the panna cotta. Then, as if offhandedly, she asks me where she can get the fruit I mentioned.

"How about I tell you as I walk you to your suite?" I offer as I get to my feet.

Shit. I'm definitely not supposed to know she got herself a suite instead of a cabin, but I guess the idea of us walking together has distracted her enough that she doesn't question my odd omniscience.

So, we walk and I talk, and it might be my imagination, but I catch her looking at my hand a few times, as though she is on the verge of holding it, like she did on the way from that bar to my bed.

Fuck me. I'm glad Sophia is facing forward and that I bought out all the surrounding suites. It's made our chances of bumping into someone—and therefore someone seeing how hard I am—negligible.

"—and the season for leechee starts around May," I say as we reach her door. "Just like with the others, you can find the best ones in Chinatown."

When she notices that I've stopped by the correct door, she frowns, so I pretend to want to go further. She visibly relaxes and says, "Wait. This is my door."

"Ah," I say, feigning surprise. "I'm right next door." I point at the suite that I carefully chose to occupy—one that I now think might be too close to hers for my sanity.

"Oh." She frowns at this "coincidence."

"I asked the agent for the suite with the most

panoramic view," I say. "He told me that that one was already booked, but that mine would be the next best thing."

This seems to mollify her, or at least I assume that's why she doesn't look suspicious anymore.

In fact, I don't understand her current expression. Or I do, but I must be mistaken.

The hooded eyes.

The parted lips.

The blush and the subtle flicker of her tongue wetting said lips.

My cock, already at attention, gives her a salute worthy of a five-star general.

"I guess I'd better head in," she murmurs but doesn't move.

I face her, which is a mistake because I get caught by the gravity exuded by her... and her delicious breasts. "Thank you for having dinner with me."

"No problem," she says breathily. "Strangely, I had a good time."

"Me too. Except I don't think there was anything strange about it."

"Well, I'd better head in," she says again... but still doesn't move.

She moistens those lips one time too many, and something inside me snaps.

Leaning down, I claim her lips in a kiss that I've been dreaming about for weeks.

Chapter 20

Sophia

I know Mason is just kissing me, but I feel on the verge of an orgasm.

I blame all the build-up. The way he smelled during dinner, the way he looked at me, and particularly the way he flashed me his fist so many times—as if on purpose—turned my brain into a panna cotta.

Wait a second.

Why am I letting this happen?

I shouldn't.

But it feels so good. His lips are soft, but the rest of him is hard. Speaking of hard, Uber is pressing against my belly, making my insides flip.

But no.

Unlike on F-Day, alcohol won't be able to serve as an excuse today. If I go through with this, I will have slept with him of my own free will.

Then again, many philosophers don't believe in free will. Many consider it an illusion.

No.

Free will is real, or else I would not be able to summon mine and use it to push Mason away from me —even though I desperately don't want to.

"Are you going to invite me in?" His eyes are wild, his breathing shallow.

I manage a shake of my head.

"You sure?"

No, I'm not sure. But I intend to fake it until I make it. "Is this your way of trying to sweet-talk me into selling you the team?"

He frowns, the wildness in his eyes dimming. "What?"

"Isn't that why you're on the cruise? To get me to sell you the team… by any means necessary?" And hey, if I had a cock like Uber, I could probably get women to sell me whatever team I wanted, be it hockey, basketball, or toe wrestling.

Mason steps back and looks like I've slapped him. "Look, Ladybug… Yes, I'm on the cruise to try to talk to you about selling, but what happened after the bar that night had nothing to do with that, and if—"

"That's a lie," I interject forcefully. "You gave me the tickets to the game as part of your quest to get me to sell. If it weren't for that, I wouldn't have ended up at that bar and F-Day wouldn't have happened."

"F-Day?"

Shit. I shouldn't have shared that moniker. "It doesn't matter what I call it. It's not happening again.

But even if it were to happen, it wouldn't help your cause. You're not *that* good."

Actually, he's very close to *that* good. I just have more experience with deceitful seducers than the average person.

Mason's expression turns thunderous. I guess that was a hit below the belt.

"You know what? Fuck this," he growls. "Don't sell me the fucking team. I don't give a shit. But at least sell to someone else."

I draw back. "Why?"

"You don't exactly have the best track record when it comes to financial matters."

My pulse spikes as I process what he's implying. "I what?"

He winces. "Never mind. That's not what I meant to say. Look, the truth is, the owner's job is challenging even for people in the hockey industry. Since you—"

Keeping him under an unblinking glare, I tune out the rest of his words as a few little things that had bothered me through the night click into place. That "track record" bit is a dig at my abysmal credit score, which he isn't supposed to know about. He also knew which suite door was mine, then pretended not to, and before that, he knew my major—even though I don't think I ever told him about that.

"—not to mention experience managing large budgets, understanding regulations, and—"

"You had me investigated, didn't you?" I poke him in the chest with an accusatory finger. His muscles feel like steel, but for a change, this doesn't make me want to drop my panties right here in the hallway.

Mason sighs. "You wouldn't even talk to me. I was desperate."

He admits it! I thought maybe I was just being paranoid. My whole body flushes with heat—and not the way it did just a few moments ago. This time, it's not the idiotically misguided arousal but an anger so righteous it could quote biblical verses... in tongues.

"You're a stalker," I hiss at him. "And I want you off this cruise."

He curls his hand inward, like he's on the verge of making a damned fist again. "Sell the team, and I'll get off at the next port."

"No." I'm so pissed I feel like a vein may pop in my brain.

Mason grimaces. "In that case, my answer is also *no*."

"Fine," I grit out. "Then I'll get off."

He shrugs, which probably means that he'll end up on the same plane as me, likely as my seatmate.

"As soon as I'm back on land, I'm going to get a restraining order," I warn.

"The first stop on this cruise is a Royal Ruskovian private island," he says. "I doubt they have a police department."

I take a deep breath and remind myself that I'm a pacifist, and more importantly, that hitting is morally wrong, no matter how tempting. Instead, I turn on my heel and angrily wave the card to my suite over the lock, then rip at the door handle.

Nothing happens.

Seething, I slam the card against the reader, again to no avail.

"You have to tap it," Mason says.

I tap the damned thing, but still no luck.

"Tap gentler and wait until you see the light flash green," Mason says with the most irritating calmness. "Then turn the handle."

I do as he says, and my anger doubles when it works.

Once in the suite, I bang the door shut so hard it's a marvel it doesn't go flying off the hinges. I take a few deep breaths and step out onto my balcony, but unlike the door, I feel unhinged, so not even the gorgeous view is relaxing me. Fuming, I grab my phone to call Abigail and vent, but then I recall my stupid decision to have a digital detox—and I don't feel like dealing with buying onboard Wi-Fi right now.

Grr.

The nerve of that guy.

It's bad enough he's stalked me and followed me onto a cruise, but to have me investigated?

I pace the room back and forth in an effort to calm down, but it's futile. The fact that he learned about my shitty credit—and then made those assumptions—is what really pisses me off. Mom really did a number on my score, and Rupert finished it off.

I groan. The idea that Mason knows about what happened with Rupert—even indirectly—makes me want to jump into the ocean and swim to the nearest shore.

No.

Screw that.

I'd sooner toss Mason overboard than let him ruin this vacation for me.

Yeah.

I again step out onto the balcony, determinedly splaying out on the comfortable chaise and forcing myself to enjoy the view.

I'm not sure if it's a food coma from all that dessert, or if I'm better at this relaxation thing than I thought, but my strategy works a little too well in that before I know it, I'm fast asleep.

———

I wake up to a sunrise over the ocean, feeling way more chilled out.

Should I sell my mansion and permanently live on a ship? No, bad idea. My staff would lose their jobs, the tortoises would lose their home, and my chances of diarrhea (courtesy of norovirus) would skyrocket.

Despite that last thought, my stomach rumbles.

Huh. Even after that huge dinner, I'm ravenous.

I head over to the washroom, and while I go about my business, I mull over a big problem: I need a way to eat without bumping into Mason, at whom I'm still pissed, gorgeous sunrise or no.

Well, he's probably already had breakfast—and has since jogged, lifted weights, and drunk wheatgrass juice or whatever. But in case he has slept in—or is up to stalking me again—he'll probably expect me at the restaurant from last night, so I'll go to the VIP restaurant instead, the one open only to the people staying in the suites.

I dress up extra nicely, for myself, not certain stalkers. True, I don't wear anything with buttons, but that's just because there might be someone else with koumpounophobia.

I grin. I know enough about the Greek language to know that koumpouno means "to button," but the origin for it is the ancient Greek word for bean— which, ironically, seems to be the cornerstone of Mason's diet.

Dammit. Why is he on my mind again?

I blame the hunger... for breakfast foods, that is. Like sausage. Or a banana—though it being fruit would remind me of a certain someone. And its shape would, too.

Grr.

Mentally smacking myself, I head over to the restaurant, and when I enter, I find it empty... except for one person.

Mason Tugev, of course.

Chapter 21

Mason

"Hello, Ladybug," I say. "Join me for breakfast." She shakes her head, but her eyes dart to the sugar porn that is the buffet at this place—as I hoped they might.

"Please," I say. "Give me a chance to apologize."

She storms over, eyes slitty. "Apologize for what?"

"The stalking," I say earnestly. "I shouldn't have done it. If someone had done it to me, I'd be as upset as you." And if they'd happened to be male, they'd be in a hospital recovery room, but I'd better not give Sophia that idea.

She seems to be at a loss for words, which must be a first for her, and maybe for philosophy majors in general.

"I also wanted to tell you something," I say. "Something I guarantee you want to know." Actually, I have two such morsels of information, and it's a wonder I didn't need to use either of them last night because I fully expected to have to.

"Tell me what?"

She asks the question with feigned nonchalance, but I can see her curiosity is as aroused as my cock is at the sight of her.

I gesture at the table in front of me and smile as if this isn't a strategic move to earn her forgiveness.

"It had better be something interesting." She grabs a plate and fills it with enough sugar to make even Buddy the Elf sick.

Setting her plate at my table, she tells the waitress taking our drink orders that she wants a chocolate mocha and looks at me as if she dares me to say something disapproving.

"Can I taste it?" I ask Sophia when the waitress leaves.

Her cheeks turning red, she glares at me. "Taste what?"

"The mocha." I suppress a chuckle that almost sends my tomato juice up my nose. "What did you think I meant?"

She turns redder than my juice, confirming that she thought I wanted to taste her. The thought of it makes me hard... or more accurately, *harder*.

"Sorry." I grin, feeling anything but. "I meant the coffee, of course. I was just reading an article about how good coffee is for one's health—assuming you only drink it before noon." And don't have milk and sugar in it, but saying that would sour this particular olive branch.

She snorts. "Is that reverse psychology?"

I cock my head. "What do you mean?"

"You say something that's bad for me is a health food and hope I won't want it anymore. Or do the reverse and claim that kale rots your teeth."

"No. Coffee really *is* good for you. Why wouldn't it be? It's a bean. It's already known to help athletic and cognitive performance, but as it turns out, it also protects against chronic diseases and lowers the risk of cancer."

"Huh."

"And so, I've been meaning to try it," I say.

"Wait." She stares at me incredulously. "You've never had coffee?"

Great. Another one. Like I haven't already been teased endlessly about this by my teammates.

I shake my head. "I tasted espresso when I was a kid, and it was bitter, so I didn't see the need to do it again… until that article."

She considers this for a second. "I had the same experience with beer and also haven't had any since then."

Huh. "Maybe people should give kids things that they don't want them to consume later in life." Like sugar, I almost say, but stop myself in time.

"It would have to be a bitter substance," she reminds me. "Else the plan might backfire."

Shit. So my sugar idea is a bust anyway. "I can't

think of many things that are bitter and bad for you. Beer might be the only one, actually."

"What about chocolate?" she says.

"If it's dark, it's good for you," I say. "I put some on my salads."

She blinks at me. "Dark chocolate... on salad?"

"Why not?"

She shrugs. "I guess it's not all that different from putting chocolate into mole sauce. But still. Sounds obscene."

"It's delicious, I assure you," I say. "Or I put it into my smoothies instead."

"Smoothies, of course." She shakes her head. "The closest I've gotten to one of those is a slushy."

I don't take the bait. "I'm sure the chef could make one for you."

She looks around. "Speaking of chefs and restaurants, why did you come here? I thought you'd be at the one from last night."

"I figured you'd think that, which is why I came here." And got the chef to make me this tofu scramble I'm currently enjoying, one which looks enough like an egg scramble to avoid a repeat of the perilous diet-related conversation—a strategy that clearly didn't bear any fruit.

Sophia gestures around the place. "Where is everyone?"

I might as well rip off that Band-Aid. "I wanted us to have privacy regardless of which restaurant we ate at, so I booked all the suites."

Her eyes widen. "All of them?"

"Yes."

She thoughtfully bites into the healthiest item on her plate: a blueberry tart. "You spent a fortune just to talk to me."

I nod.

"I guess I could've avoided this if I hadn't dodged your calls," she says after a pause.

"True, but you have the right not to talk to me. I'm in the wrong... but I appreciate you saying that."

She cocks her head. "So, back to the information you bribed me with?"

"What about it?" I look at our non-empty plates.

"Can you tell me what it is? I'll stick around here until the end of breakfast. I promise."

I tsk-tsk. "You'd make a bad hockey strategist."

"I'll take that as a compliment." She tosses a tiny muffin at me, which I catch and set back on her plate before putting on my best poker face—something I do during critical game moments.

"If you want the info early, you'll have to go on an excursion with me," I say.

She purses her lips and looks thoughtful. Meanwhile, her drink comes, and she pushes it toward me.

I take a tiny sip and can't help but flinch.

"What?" she demands.

"I think they forgot to add coffee to all that sugar." I take a gulp of tomato juice to get the treacle taste out of my mouth. "But hey, at least it wasn't even remotely bitter."

She samples the drink and sighs. "If you ask me, this needs another spoonful of sugar. What's the excursion?"

I shrug. "Anything involving nature. You pick."

She arches an eyebrow.

All right. The best way for me to make up for my invasion of her privacy is to share something embarrassing about myself. "They didn't have any nature documentaries on the TV in my room, and I need my nature fix."

She cocks her head. "You like nature shows?"

"Love them."

I prepare for the onslaught of the usual jokes, but she just smiles approvingly. "You'd probably enjoy visiting my mansion."

"On account of the tortoises?"

She purses her lips. "Your dossier on me is that thorough?"

I shake my head. "I knew about Donatello and April before we met. Theodore showed them to me."

"Oh. You guys hung out?" Is that a hint of jealousy in her voice?

"We didn't hang out that much, but when he heard about my fondness for all things nature, he had me visit his sanctuary, and I had a nice chat with Dr. Kelpcon." Or it was nice until it started to seem like she wanted to use me for some sort of human breeding experiment...

involving the two of us. Oh, and what made that last bit worse was that her flirtations coincided with the moment I noticed the white buttons on her lab coat.

Sophia waggles her eyebrows. "Did Dr. Kelpcon tell you all about Donatello's sexual prowess?"

I grin. "She did, but she also shared some fun facts I didn't previously know, like how those tortoises have lungs on their back."

Sophia crosses her arms in front of her chest. "She never told *me* that." She bites her lip. "I think it's my lack of a big cock."

I arch an eyebrow.

She blushes again. "I meant Donatello, not you."

"Huh?"

She looks at me pleadingly. "Can we move on?"

I resist the urge to smile. "The lungs in question are just under the shell, so if you scare a tortoise, it will hide inside with a loud hiss."

"Huh." Sophia grabs a muffin absentmindedly. "April did hiss at me the other day, when I accidentally snuck up on her."

"There you go."

She munches on that muffin so seductively I stare at my plate to maintain my equilibrium.

"What else did the good doctor tell you?" she asks.

"She told me about the birds that ride your tortoises." Having recovered somewhat, I look back at her, just in time to see her lick crumbs from her lips, which makes the aforementioned cock way bigger.

Because I'm pretty sure she was *not* talking about Donatello.

"Ah, right." Sophia chuckles, her blush almost gone. "According to Dr. Kelpcon, the birds and the tortoises have a symbiotic relationship. Something about ticks in the folds of tortoise skin."

Whew. The phrase "the folds of tortoise skin" settles my dick... a little. "If you ask me, you have much more of a symbiotic relationship with those tortoises than the birds do. They need someone to pay rent, and you oblige."

"And what do I get?" She picks up a mini-doughnut. "The junk I eat doesn't include ticks."

Is she serious? "You get to feel the relaxation from watching them." I sure would.

Her cheeks flush again. "Those lovebirds—or love tortoises—hump way too much for me to be able to relax around them."

At the mention of humping, my eyes get drawn to her cleavage, ending my cock's brief reprieve.

"So... what was that bargaining chip of information?" she asks, shifting in her seat.

Ah. Right. "Mr. Berger is alive and well."

She stares at me in confusion.

"You wanted to know if he made it," I remind her.

"I did?"

I sigh. "The guy whose life we saved." I'm being generous when I include her in that "we."

"Oh. The hairy guy who was having a heart attack?"

"His name, as it turns out, is Hampton Berger, and he's made a complete recovery," I say. What I don't mention is that our shared lawyer wasn't going to divulge this to either of us, so I used my own channels to find out —the same Max Stolyar who gave me the dossier on her.

"Hampton Berger?" She chuckles. "Do you think his friends call him Ham?"

"Ham Berger?"

"Hey," she says. "He survived, so it's not in poor taste."

"Not in poor taste? That heart attack might've been the result of eating too many hamburgers. Besides, should someone with the last name Papachristodoulopoulou really be throwing stones?"

Her eyes widen. "You said that correctly."

"Why wouldn't I?" All it took was a lesson with a private speech coach who's fluent in Greek—no biggie.

"Very few people are able to do that," she says. "Until now, it was just my butler who could. Not a single professor can do it in school."

"A shame for those so-called philosophy professors. Greek to them should be what Latin is to Catholic priests."

She smiles. "I believe they do the Mass in English nowadays."

"Ah. Right." I shouldn't have used an example related to religion—it makes my parents spring to mind.

"Are you okay?" she asks, her eyebrows pleating in a

small frown. She must've picked up on my change in mood.

Should I tell her about my parents? I feel like I owe it to her after everything. But no. I can't. There's a reason I've never told anyone. Not to mention, it's not a fair trade. All I learned about her from the investigation is ultimately minutia: where she goes to school, her credit score, and her plans to go on this cruise. Max didn't tell me anything deeper, and nothing like her most painful secret. Not that I think she even has such a thing, given how cheerful she—

"Mason Tugev!" slurs a vaguely familiar accented voice. "As I live and breathe. It *is* you."

I spin in my seat and take in a super-thin guy in a rumpled uniform, a bottle of vodka in his hand and two liters on his breath.

Sophia gives me a questioning look, and I shrug, as confused as she is.

"It is I," the guy says after a hiccup. "Your biggest fan."

Well, that explains why he's here.

"Hi," I say in the friendliest tone I can muster—because you have to be nice to the fans. "It's a pleasure to meet you." As much of a pleasure as it'd be to search for alcoholic ticks in the folds of a drunken tortoise's skin.

"Wait, you don't recognize me?" He slams his vodka on the table and extends his cadaver-like hand to me. "I am Ivan Vorobey."

Sophia's eyes widen, so I start to suspect he's a

celebrity of some kind, but I don't have any clue as to how I know him. I mean, I'd remember that name: if translated from Russian, it's Jack Sparrow, which is the name of the pirate played by—

"He's the captain," Sophia says, just as I was about to make that leap. She lowers her voice and leans closer to me. "And he's drinking."

Ivan gestures at his bottle dismissively. "Just a little digestif after breakfast."

He takes my water glass, spills its contents on the floor, then fills it to the brim with vodka. "Have a shot with me," he says. "To honor our meeting."

"Sorry, I can't drink that," I say.

"Stomach ulcer?" he asks in a horrified whisper usually reserved for discussing conditions like cancer. "It happened to my old man. The doctors forbade him to drink." He shudders. "I believe you can still take your vodka rectally, but my papa refused that option, worried it would make him gay."

There's a lot to unpack there, but I simply push the vodka away and, keeping my tone fan-friendly, I say, "My coach forbade me—and I respect him more than any doctor." It's not even a complete lie: Coach always tells us not to binge drink, and such a "shot" would qualify as that. More importantly, I need to stay sharp to keep up with Sophia.

"But of course! Of course." Ivan downs the glass he poured for me in one long gulp. "One should always listen to one's captain, coach, wife, and mistress."

I can tell that Sophia, like me, is wondering if he

means the BDSM-type of mistress or the woman he's cheating on his wife with.

"So," Ivan says. "I wanted to ask you about that game where you scored three goals."

Fuck. I look at Sophia for help, but she's clearly still holding a grudge because she says, "Ah. Great. You boys have your talk. I'm going to go select that excursion."

"Thanks," I grumble.

"No problem." She leaps to her feet, blows me a sarcastic goodbye kiss, and departs, leaving behind a faint scent of mango and watermelon.

I turn to Ivan. "Can you be a little more specific?"

He pours himself another glass of vodka. "What do you mean?"

"I've scored a hat trick in many games."

"Ah." He downs the drink. "I mean the one where you punched that guy. And that other guy."

I suppress a sigh. This is going to be a very long morning.

Chapter 22

Sophia

Having booked the excursion, I stroll in Central Park and ponder why and how I've managed to forgive Mason so quickly. Because somehow, I have done just that, and I don't think he deserves it.

Am I being shallow? Am I letting him get away with murder because of his looks?

Maybe. Then again, he did apologize. And he found out about the hamburger guy for me. Not to mention, he also saved said guy's life in the first place. I just have to make sure not to go any further than mere forgiveness when—

"Ladybug," Mason says, jogging up to me without panting in the slightest. "What fun activity did you book for us?"

"Hey." I was half expecting the good captain to be permanently attached to Mason at the hip, but he's missing. "Do you like sea life?"

He nods enthusiastically. "Are we going snorkeling?"

"No." I'm not so foolish as to expose myself to the sight of him wearing only swim trunks. That way lies a repeat of F-Day, or worse. "As soon as we reach the next port, we're taking a ride on a glass-bottom boat." Doing my best to simulate the salesy tone of the concierge, I say, "It's like wearing a diving mask while staying dry."

Because if Mason gets wet, so will I.

"That's great," he says. "We could probably catch sight of coral, fish, seaweed, or maybe even a shipwreck."

"Speaking of shipwrecks," I say. "Where's the good captain?"

"You mean the not-so-good captain?" Mason smiles wryly. "He drank so much I wouldn't trust him with a paper ship."

"I know, right?" I say as his smile flutters something in my belly.

I mean, no, it doesn't. This is fear for my life, given the captain situation.

Mason extends his elbow to me, but I hesitate.

"I'm not sure if it will make you feel better," he says. "But I confronted him about the drinking, and he assured me that he has a high tolerance and that, and I quote, 'it would take a lot more than *that* to get me ship faced.'"

"How reassuring." I slide my hand into the crook of

his elbow—but only because ignoring it is awkward. The action is a mistake, though, because feeling his hard bicep intensifies the "fear for life" flutters.

Mason acts like my hand on his arm was a foregone conclusion. "What might be more reassuring is this factoid: he doesn't actually drive the ship like you would a car. He uses navigation systems like radar, GPS, and autopilot. More importantly, a team of officers and experienced crew members operates those systems. Many of them are from India, and they are, to quote Jack Sparrow again, 'Teetotalers with too many PhDs.'"

"Jack Sparrow?"

"His name translated from Russian," he explains.

I squeeze his arm. "You speak Russian?"

"Enough to translate that name," he says.

"That's crazy. Despite taking two years of Spanish in school, I can only say a few phrases. And I only know a few words in Greek."

This last bit reminds me unpleasantly of my mom. Strangely, Mason's bicep tenses in my grasp, as if the topic offends him. Yet when he speaks, his tone is bland.

"Most Estonians know some Russian," he says.

"Ah. Is it the language your parents speak?"

He comes to a jarring halt and frees his arm from my touch. "Did you feel that?"

I frown. "Feel what?"

"The ship stopped."

As if to confirm his words, the intercom comes to life, and the cruise director welcomes us to go ashore.

"Where do you want to meet?" Masons asks as soon as the announcement is over.

"At the entrance to the port?" I'm still confused by his behavior.

"Right," he says. "See you there."

With that, he jogs away without a second glance.

Only after he is gone do I realize that the weirdness coincided with my bringing up the topic of his parents.

When I meet Mason down by the port entrance, he seems fine.

More than fine.

He's changed his shirt for a tight muscle tee and his trousers for swim trunks, a combo that is unfairly distracting.

"Where do we board the glass-bottom boat?" he asks, looking around with curiosity.

"There." I point at a boat that looks like a children's toy next to the *Wonder of the Oceans*.

Mason cocks his head. "I'm not sure I'm going to fit inside such a small space."

I have no idea why that statement makes my cheeks burn, but it does. "Luckily, your ego doesn't take up any space, so we should be fine."

"Touché." He extends his elbow for me once more

and—purely out of expediency—I put my hand on his bicep and lead him to our destination.

Hmm. As we get on board, I realize our ride-to-be isn't just small in proportion to the cruise liner. It's small when compared to other large things, like, say, Uber.

"Did you book up the whole boat?" Mason asks, scanning the empty seats. "I thought that was my move."

"No, I didn't." I guess this excursion didn't appeal to anyone else.

Oops. Spoke too soon.

An older couple walks on holding hands, the wife smiling like her life depends on it and the husband looking like he's just swallowed a rotten lemon.

"Hi," says the woman with a Southern drawl. "I'm Martha, and this here is Andrew."

Andrew grunts something in a heavy Brooklyn accent.

"Hello," Mason says in an unusually friendly tone. "Come sit next to us. Sophia here has been wanting to chat with perfect strangers."

Is that a dig at my desire to eat at the shared tables on the cruise, or a genuine wish to help? It's hard to tell with this guy.

"Hi." I extend my hand to each of the newcomers. "As Mason said, I'm Sophia. We're both from New York."

"I'm also from New York," says Andrew, and I don't point out that I could've guessed based on his accent.

"But now he lives in Florida," Martha says. "With me and our sixteen Siberian huskies."

Sixteen?

If his arching eyebrow is any indicator, Mason is also impressed with the number.

"You could run two sleds with that many." Mason scratches his head.

When we all look at him questioningly, he explains, "Dog sledding is a popular activity in Estonia."

Ah. Right. From what little geography I know, Estonia is somewhere cold.

If Andrew and Martha have questions about Mason's motherland, they don't voice them. Instead, they look warily out the window in time to see our little boat begin moving.

Following their gaze makes me feel odd, so I look at the main attraction of this excursion, the glass bottom.

Except there isn't much to see yet.

Crap.

I hope something shows up and soon.

Our boat picks up speed, and I wish it hadn't. I can feel it moving a lot more than I could feel the cruise ship. Come to think of it, on the cruise ship, I hardly noticed that it was sailing at all.

When I glance up from the glass bottom, I find Martha and Andrew looking uncomfortable, so I make conversation by asking no one in particular, "Huskies like the cold, right?"

Martha narrows her eyes at me. "What are you trying to say?"

"Our dogs are very happy," Andrew says challengingly. "They like the sunshine."

Are they protesting too much?

"Huskies have a double coat," Mason chimes in. "It helps with the cold, but in a pinch, it can also protect from the heat. Still, I doubt they should overexercise outside in the Florida sun."

"They are happy," Martha hisses. "Happy, I tell you."

Oh, crap. What did we say?

"We have the AC set to sixty-five for them," Andrew says. "They never overheat."

"Okay. Cool." I smile weakly. "No pun intended."

Ignoring me, Martha whispers something into her husband's ear.

Looking like the lemon he ate has suddenly became sourer, Andrew stands up and clears his throat. "I'd feel more comfortable if I sat over by the entrance," he says. "Come, honey."

They both get up, clearly eager to be as far away from us—or me—as possible.

Note to self: when meeting people with dogs, never ask any questions, or else.

Crap.

As I watch the couple's wobbly gait, something quivers in my stomach, and I don't mean the guilt about the social faux pas.

"How was that?" Mason whispers sarcastically when the Floridians are out of earshot. "You sure you're still upset I deprived you of more of the same back on the cruise?"

I shrug, then point down. "I see something."

The something is less murky waters that get bluer and more see-through by the minute. Soon, the view becomes actually interesting, or as interesting as fish, seaweed, and coral can be.

Then again, going by the expression on Mason's face, you'd think we were watching an action-packed summer blockbuster.

Suddenly, I hear a retching sound.

Oh, no.

Andrew leaps to his feet and runs out to the deck, with Martha after him.

Something they ate? Norovirus? Either way, I hope they're not on our cruise.

But no.

I realize that I've been feeling progressively woozy myself. I just haven't allowed myself to dwell on it... but it's getting harder to ignore by the second.

It's a feeling a lot like my post F-Day hangover. Only my world is spinning more right now, and the nausea is sharper. Not to mention, I have a desperate desire to be on dry land that wasn't part of my post F-Day experience.

"Are you okay?" Mason asks, sounding worried.

"Sure." I take a deep breath. "Why do you ask?"

"You're looking kind of green."

"I'm fine." I make the mistake of looking out the window, and as soon as I see the ocean move, my seasickness intensifies.

I suck in a couple more deep breaths.

"You don't look fine," Mason says.

"I could use some fresh air." Except I feel bad interrupting his nature-show-like fun.

"Great idea." He helps me get up. "Let's get you some."

We walk out onto the deck, and at first, the fresh air seems to help, but then I overhear sounds from another part of the boat that remind me of the projectile-vomiting scene from *The Exorcist*.

"Fuck," Mason growls. "You want to go back?"

I shake my head and swallow the drool pooling unpleasantly in my mouth.

"Here." He takes off his shirt, wets it using the water from his bottle, and presses the cold compress against my forehead.

Okay. Between seeing shirtless Mason and the cold, I feel a tiny bit better, but then the sounds resume, ruining everything.

I can't even tell who is making the sounds at this point: Martha, Andrew, or—most likely—Pazuzu, the demon antagonist from *The Exorcist*.

Mason looks at me worriedly as I feel Pazuzu slither into my own body and use his gnarly fingers to squeeze the nausea center in my brain. Heaving, I bend over the railing so fast Mason must think I want to fall overboard. He grabs me with a strong grip, but then Pazuzu's possession takes hold and he switches to holding my hair.

Fuck me. I'm going to die. My insides are coming

out of my mouth. It goes on and on until I feel like my spleen is swimming with the fishes.

When it's over, I finally feel a little better. But I'm mortified, even more so than the time I reached into a sample box next to a doughnut shop, only to realize it wasn't a sample box. The woman holding said box was a doughnut shop employee on her break, and the box was her lunch.

"Drink." Mason extends his water bottle to me, his expression worried instead of grossed out.

"You'll have to burn this bottle," I mutter.

"Stop being silly and drink." He thrusts the bottle into my hands.

Fine. I force myself to take a sip. Then another.

"Good job," Mason says. "Now look toward the distant horizon."

I do so, and that helps a little more.

"Stand here." Mason moves me over a few feet, arranging me in such a way that I feel wind on my face.

Yeah. That's better—except the sounds resume.

"Don't worry," Mason says. "I've got this."

He's got what? Holy water?

To my shock, Mason starts singing at the top of his lungs. The song is in a language I don't recognize— perhaps Russian or Estonian. It's slow and repetitive, and Mason sings offkey, but he does a great job of drowning out the sounds of Pazuzu. Combined with the horizon watching and the wind on my face, it makes me feel almost human.

After about a minute, Mason stops singing, and I hear someone ask, "Should we head back?"

It's the boat's captain. Unlike our cruise ship's counterpart, he doesn't look drunk out of his mind.

"Yes, fucking please," Mason barks. "Get her to the shore as soon as possible—and sail smoothly from now on, or I'll rip off your arm."

Rip off his arm? Sounds like something a Viking would say... and I shouldn't find it hot. At all. I'm a pacifist, or so I thought. Also, is it even possible to sail smoothly? Not sure, but given the frightened expression on the captain's face, he'll certainly give it his best.

As Mason turns back to me, his fierce expression morphs back into worry, and he resumes his singing—just in time too, as Pazuzu attempts to possess me again.

After what feels like four hours of torture, we dock and Mason carries me off the boat clasped against his chest like a bride. I'm so nauseated that I don't even find the strength to protest. All I can do is pant, "Don't take me back on any ships. I'm not ready."

"Of course. Want to sit on that bench?" He gestures at one that is so far away I wouldn't even see the ocean from it—a huge plus at the moment.

I nod. "Let's swing by the bathroom first, please."

By now, I'm pretty sure I can stand on my own two feet, but he carries me there anyway. He's about to step inside the ladies' room with me when I finally find my spine.

"I can use the bathroom by myself," I say, wriggling free. "Thank you."

He sets me down and watches skeptically as I take a few (admittedly unsteady) steps.

"I'll be fine." Thrusting his wet shirt that had been my compress back at him, I hurry into the bathroom.

Damn. When I check myself out in the mirror, I'm paler than the nearby toilet. Oh, well. I do my business, wash my face with hand soap, and then do my best to make myself as presentable as is possible after a Pazuzu attack.

When I walk out, Mason has his shirt back on—a pity. He's also holding his phone to his ear, and his back is to me, so he doesn't realize I'm behind him.

No idea why, but I softly approach to listen in on his conversation—only to realize that if our roles were reversed, I'd call it stalking behavior and never let him forget it.

"Sure, tickets for your wife and mistress as well," Mason says, and I exhale a breath I didn't realize I was holding. A part of me thought that he might be speaking to either a wife or a girlfriend that he never mentioned, but it's unlikely either of those entities would have a wife and a mistress—not unless she was especially French.

"But," Mason continues, "in that case, you'll have to delay departure by three hours."

Oh. Is he talking to the—

"Thanks, Ivan," Mason says, confirming my guess. "After the game, I'll sign the puck for you."

I can tell he's about to hang up, so I tiptoe backward to the bathroom so that it looks like I'm just exiting by the time he turns my way.

"Hey." Approaching me, he unceremoniously picks me up again and carries me to the distant bench. "How do you feel?"

Now that I'm not sick, his touch sends tendrils of heat into all my secret places—but I'm not about to admit that. Instead, I swallow and say huskily, "Better."

I'm also touched that he'd go through the trouble of stalling the cruise for me, but I don't tell him that either in case he's about to use it as a bargaining chip to get me to sell the team. More importantly, I'm not about to admit that I eavesdropped—I enjoy my position of high moral ground too much for that.

"Just sit, breathe, and relax." He lowers me onto the bench and sits next to me, draping his arm across my shoulders.

This is nice... but it's too much like being at the movies with my sweetheart, so I should tell him to stop.

Any moment now.

Then again, his arm is somehow helping me recover, which I think justifies allowing the embrace for a little bit longer.

For a couple of minutes. Or a dozen minutes.

He also smells really good, like a winter forest. There is such a thing as aroma therapy, so I just inhale deeper and let myself enjoy it.

He glances at me and nods approvingly. "Your color is returning."

Maybe. Or maybe it's the foundation I applied while I was in the bathroom. "What was the song you sang to me?"

He abruptly removes the comfort of his arm, and through the wet tank, I can see his muscles tensing. "Estonian Lullaby. My mother would sing it to me when I was little."

Oh, shit. I think I finally get it. "Something happened to her, didn't it?"

Mason's expression turns stormy. "No."

"Oh." What then? Because his parents seem to be a touchy subject, to say the least.

I must be staring at him expectantly because he scrubs a rough hand over his face and blows out a breath before looking away. When he looks back at me, his expression is carefully blank. "My mother and father are alive and well," he says evenly.

I bite my lip. I can still sense something there, and some devil prods me to ask, "Did your dossier mention *my* mother?"

He shakes his head. "It really wasn't as in depth as you think. Mainly, I learned your credit score, how much income you had prior to your inheritance, and most importantly, the places where I might bump into you."

Oh. So... nothing about Rupert. A huge weight lifts off my shoulders. I'd rather puke in front of Mason a dozen more times than have him learn about how I was duped like a lovesick fool. I do feel the urge to tell him something more, though—if only because I'm certain there is something complicated going on between him and his parents... just like between my mother and me.

"When I turned eighteen, my mother opened a bunch of credit cards in my name and used the money to pay for her drug addiction," I say, matching his even tone. I don't know why, but I don't find this as embarrassing as the Rupert situation—maybe because in this case, I didn't participate in my own destruction. "Needless to say," I continue. "We're no longer on speaking terms."

Mason's hard features soften. He takes my hand and gives it a reassuring squeeze that is a touch too hard. "I'm so sorry. I know exactly how you feel."

"You do?" I stare at him.

Mason's jaw tenses. "What I am about to tell you, I've never told anyone."

I don't blink. I even momentarily stop breathing.

"My parents do not want me in their life." The words are loaded with so much pain my throat burns on his behalf. "Remember when I told you how Estonia is the least religious country in the world? Well, as irony would have it, my parents found religion and turned into the kind of zealots who give you two choices: join us or we never want to see you again."

That is the last thing I expected to hear.

Speechless, I gape at him.

"I actually tried. Went to services with them and read their holy books—but of course, enthusiasm is very difficult to fake. It didn't help that they thought I was up to 'debauchery' based on the bullshit they read about me in the tabloids. Even if the stories were true, for them to judge me is hypocritical to say the least— my father used to drink more vodka than our captain, and my mom had at least two affairs that I know of. But anyway, eventually they sat me down and told me they decided it would be best for them if they didn't have a son, and requested I never call or visit."

This time, I'm the one who grabs his hand. It's ice cold, so I rub it between my palms, using friction to return some warmth to his skin.

"I'm so sorry," I say earnestly. "And I hope you realize that it's their loss."

And I mean it, too. He's an attractive, successful, wealthy man who is, some stalking aside, also genuinely nice. At least insofar as taking care of a seasick woman. Or saving a man's life.

Yeah, that last one is kind of a biggie.

"Same goes for you," he says. "Your mother is the one missing out."

I swallow a sudden knot in my throat. "Yeah, sure."

"I mean it," he says.

I sigh. "Rationally, I know that's true, but I often feel shitty regardless." And have issues that led to me ending up with someone like Rupert.

"I understand." He covers my hands with his. "Just like how I know that someone else won't hurt me in the same way my parents did, but I still often feel like they might."

Trust issues. Should I tell him that could be my middle name?

"Is this why you haven't had a serious relationship?" I blurt, then wince at my own awkward bluntness. "I'm asking on behalf of all your rabid fans." Nope, that didn't make it better.

He arches an eyebrow. "So... you looked me up?"

He told me he doesn't date, but I wanted to dig deeper into it. "It's not stalking," I say defensively. "You're a public figure."

He sighs too. "I've never thought about it that way, but maybe you have a point. I certainly don't trust people easily... but I somehow feel like I can trust you. Maybe because you've told me your biggest secret?"

Except I haven't. Rupert is my biggest secret, and I haven't mentioned him.

"What about you?" Mason asks. "Have you had any serious relationships? And before you bring up the damned report I ran on you, it didn't say anything about that, or else I wouldn't ask."

If I were going to tell him about Rupert, this would be my chance. He's certainly shared something very painful and personal.

But apparently, I can't, which is why my mouth says, "No. I haven't had any serious relationships."

If I were Pinocchio, my nose would be the length of Uber.

Mason's sympathetic expression makes me feel like a piece of Pazuzu for lying. "Do you think it's because of the thing with your mom?"

I shrug. "That's what any therapist would say."

He waves his hand dismissively. "Coach made us all see one of those. She tried to seduce me."

"That bitch." Oops, that just slipped out. "I mean, seducing a patient is against all the rules."

A devilish grin twists his lips. "Are you jealous?"

"Why would I be jealous?" Seriously, I'd like to know... because I totally am.

"I don't know." He cocks his head. "It just sounds like you're jealous."

"I'm not." Time to change the subject. "Have you ever heard of the Pinocchio paradox?"

Hmm, the first thing I do after lying is mention a famous liar? Smooth.

Mason puts his arm around me again. "What, pray tell, is the Pinocchio paradox?"

"Well..." I do my best not to sound like Professor Ambien. "This paradox arises if Pinocchio ever says, 'My nose grows now.'"

Mason frowns. "Because if what he says is true and his nose is growing, that would be breaking the rule of it only growing when he lies. But if what he says is false, and his nose isn't growing, then he's telling a lie —" He rubs his temples. "This is why I'd never major in philosophy. It can give you a worse headache than a puck to the head."

"Apologies. I didn't realize that using your brain might give you a headache." I'm actually not a fan of paradoxes myself, and for similar reasons to his, but they provide a great distraction—case in point: no more talk about jealousy.

Mason rolls his eyes. "Did you know there is a Russian version of Pinocchio? His name is Buratino, and his nose is permanently long—not because he's a liar, but just because that's what the author, Tolstoy, decided. The tale is very popular in Estonia."

I gape at him. "Tolstoy? As in the guy who wrote *War and Peace*?" That would be like Disney producing *The Texas Chainsaw Massacre*, musical edition.

"No, not that one, but a distant relative of his," Mason says. "There are actually three famous Tolstoys: Lev Nikolayevich, Aleksey Nikolayevich, and Aleksey Konstantinovich."

"Not confusing at all," I say with a grin.

"Not as confusing as the Pinocchio paradox," he retorts.

"Touché." I look at the large clock above the building where the bathrooms are. "Shouldn't we head back?"

I ask for two reasons: I genuinely have no idea how long of a delay Ivan granted him, but more importantly, I'd like to see if he'll try to cash in on what he did for me.

"Oh, you didn't get the text?" he asks.

I pat my empty-of-phone pockets. "I'm on a digital detox."

He waves his phone at me. "For some reason, our departure was delayed by three hours."

Some reason? So he *isn't* taking credit, which is to

his credit. Unless... does he know that I overheard and is thus being Machiavellian?

"How do you feel?" he asks.

I scan myself for any remnants of Pazuzu, finding none. "Better. Why?"

"It might do you good to take a stroll," he says. "There's a botanical garden nearby—no ocean in sight."

"Yeah. That might be nice." The farther away I am from boats, the better.

We head out and chat about our likes and dislikes as we stroll. Turns out, we're both into video games, his favorite being a hockey game—of course—while mine is *The Talos Principle*, a philosophical puzzle game. Furthermore, we are playing the same video game franchise at the moment: *Assassin's Creed*, except my game deals with the Vikings, whereas his is set in Ancient Greece.

"Are you feeling well enough now to get back on the cruise?" he asks when we return to the garden entrance.

"Yes, I think so." As in, I completely forgot about Pazuzu.

"Which restaurant should we have dinner at?" he asks while we make our way back.

I know I should object to spending so much time together, but I don't. "How about the VIP one?"

And I'm not choosing it because it's more romantic. It's just closer to my suite, that is all.

"Good choice," Mason says. "It's Captain's Night at the other restaurant."

Hmm. This was another chance to brag about what he did for me, but he kept mum. Also—

"Does 'Captain's Night' mean everyone has to dress formally?" As in, I could see Mason wearing a suit or a tux?

"Yes." He winces. "With all those fucking buttons."

Ah. "Yeah. No. Let's stick to the VIP restaurant."

He looks relieved, which warms me for some unfathomable reason.

"So…" he says. "Is it safe to say our excursion was a bust?"

I chuckle humorlessly. "A bust would be watching some muddy water. What we had was a clusterfuck."

"In that case, I say it doesn't count, and we do something else tomorrow."

Wow.

Another date… I mean, excursion.

I want it so badly that it's scary, which might be why I say, "No. But nice try."

He turns to me, gray eyes gleaming. "Why not?"

I shrug. "We never agreed to a do-over if the glass boat ride sucked."

He nods knowingly. "What if I told you another interesting bit of information?"

There it is. Is he going to fess up about the delay now? "What kind of information?"

"Oh, it's something juicy," he says with a seductive wink. "I was going to use it the first night, to get you to stay for dinner but thankfully, I didn't have to."

Oh, so he's not coming clean. But then, what could it be? "Fine. Tell me."

"Not so fast," Mason says. "We do the excursion first; I give up the goods after—and only if it's not another clusterfuck, so choose the activity wisely."

I sigh. I hope I don't end up giving up my goods as the result of all this. Also, curiosity is killing me. "How about you tell me now, and I give you my word to do the excursion?"

"No," he says. "But nice try."

Chapter 23

Mason

For the rest of the walk and during dinner, Sophia tries to get me to tell her the secret that I dangled in front of her, but I remain strong.

"You know," I say as we finish dessert. "Until today, I thought Spike was the most curious creature on this planet, but you might give him a run for his kibble."

In fact, I bet if I had a secret juicy enough, I could get her to sell me the team... except I don't seem to care about that as much anymore.

She bats her eyelashes at me. "Curiosity is my only vice."

I scan the table with its scattered remains of dessert. "Yeah. Totally."

She stands up. "Fine. I like my sweets. And I will sleep in on occasion."

Figures. Just as I'm getting up, she mentions herself in bed, so here I am walking her to her suite with a major hard-on.

As we walk, the wind must pick up because I can feel the movement of the ship, a soft rocking underneath us. Hopefully, *she* can't feel it, and I don't tell her about it lest I trigger any sort of nocebo seasickness. I just watch her closely to see if she feels unwell—which turns out to be a mistake.

Looking at her is doing bad things to the aforementioned hard-on.

When we reach her door, she clears her throat. "Thank you. It was a nice day, all things considered."

My gaze drops to her lips, and I step closer, my heart pounding faster as her sweet scent reaches my nostrils. "Why don't we make it even nicer?"

She vehemently shakes her head. "Sorry. No. I've got to go."

With that, she slides her key over her door, but too fast again. After some fussing, she gets the door open and rushes inside as if being chased by a puck flying at a hundred miles per hour.

Fuck. Did I misread the situation so completely? I thought she would at least kiss me, but she acted like I'd contracted leprosy.

Entering my own suite, I take a cold shower—which does nothing for my Sophia-inspired lust, so I fist my cock as a plan B, thinking of her the whole time but especially when I come.

Despite all that, when I get into bed, Sophia is on my mind, and sleep refuses to come—which forces me to do something I suck at: examine my feelings.

It doesn't take me long to understand just how fucked I am.

When it comes to Sophia, buying the team isn't my main goal anymore... because I want *her* more.

I know it's stupid. She's the team owner, is much too young for me, and most importantly, she might not even want me like that—as evidenced by the kiss that never happened. What she calls F-Day might've been a drunken mistake on her part, and maybe it wasn't as good for her as it was for me—though she sure sounded like she enjoyed herself.

And here I go. Hard. Again.

Fuck me sideways.

———

In the morning, Sophia shows up for breakfast at the same restaurant as yesterday, which is a good sign. If she were looking to avoid me, she could've gone to the other restaurant—though she could've decided that I'd think she'd be elsewhere based on reverse psychology.

"Hey." She beams at me.

Okay, a smile isn't what one does when one is unhappy you guessed her whereabouts correctly.

"How'd you sleep?" she asks.

"Like a rock." As in, my cock was as hard as a rock, thanks to a certain someone and her perfect breasts.

She grabs a plate and, as expected, loads it with all the most sugar-laden options on display.

We resume some of the get-to-know-you

conversation, and among other things, I learn that she's always had trouble insulting people. I'll probably regret it later, but I offer to help her improve her skills and then teach her some of the gems from the repertoire my team and I use on the ice.

"I've thought of an activity we could do," she says when the lesson is over. "It's not watching nature, but it will happen *in* nature, a forest to be precise. I hope that's okay with you?"

As long as she's there, I don't care what we do. "Sounds mysterious. Will you tell me what it is?"

She grins at me triumphantly. "Ziplining."

Chapter 24

Sophia

"Hi, I'm Levi," says our "instructor"—a boy of about fifteen, if I'm generous. "Let me go over the safety instructions before we gear up."

He goes into a spiel that makes me wonder if he's Professor Ambien's long-lost grandson.

As my mind wanders, I return to something I've been dwelling on all morning and on the way here: the kiss that never happened last night.

There was definite disappointment—and hurt—in Mason's eyes. Also, though it could be my imagination, he's been a bit more closed off today compared to the way he was in the botanical gardens. And he hasn't looked at my boobs even once.

Maybe he misunderstood last night. I didn't want to kiss him because I suddenly felt the rocking of the ship, and I was afraid Pazuzu might yank out the dinner I'd just had. It had nothing to do with him. At all. In fact, it was scary how much I wanted to kiss him despite Pazuzu... and how much I still do, even in front of our underaged instructor and the rest of these people.

Hmm. Maybe it's for the best that we didn't kiss, even if it was due to a misunderstanding. Maybe I should—

"—and use the glove to brake."

Wait. A glove? What glove? What else did I miss?

"Now," the possible-violation-of-child-labor-laws says, "the gear is over there." He gestures at a row of harnesses and helmets.

"Hey." I tug on Mason's sleeve. "Do you know what to do?"

"Sure. It's like this." Mason grabs a harness and slips it on effortlessly, while I do my best not to gawk at the place on his crotch where the harness has created a bulge that is even bigger than the usual situation. Next, Mason grabs a helmet and slips it on—which makes him look a lot like how he did on the ice.

Hot.

"All right." I grab another harness and try to put it on... only to end up smacking my teeth with a carabiner and then nearly choking when a shoulder strap somehow becomes a noose.

"Can I help?" Levi asks, seemingly talking directly to Plato's nipple, which is hard and therefore visible through my shirt despite my bra.

Thanks, Mason's bulge.

"No," Mason growls, just as I say, "Yes."

Mason's hand curls into a fist, not helping the

nipple situation in the slightest. Levi takes a step back —a wise choice.

"If you value your hands, don't even think about touching her," Mason growls again.

Levi's recently sprouted Adam's apple bobs, and his voice goes girlishly high. "Yes, sir." Swiftly, he goes to help someone else.

"That was pretty rude," I say. "Who is going to help me now?"

With an eyeroll, Mason steps over and removes the harness from my body with the same ease as when he took off my bra and panties in my fantasy last night.

"Slide your leg in here." He holds up a loop of the harness, so I do as I'm told. "And here." I slip in my other leg, which accidentally makes his fingers brush my calf, causing me to shiver all over.

"That's it," he murmurs, then tightens the straps— which ends up doing two very noticeable things: it thrusts Socrates and Plato up better than any pushup bra and presses on my groin area in such a way that all it would take is a little jiggle for me to come.

Okay, it's official. I understand why someone would want to be on the receiving end of rope bondage. Having yourself squeezed in this way is an extremely sensuous experience... although, it is very possible that Mason's presence is as important a variable in this as the straps are.

"Is everyone ready?" Levi asks.

I'm ready for many things now, ziplining the least

of them. Alas, since climbing Mason isn't in the cards, I climb a tree instead.

Once we're up, Levi apprehensively attaches Mason to the line before gesturing at me. "I need to clip in her carabiner in the same way."

"You may do so," Mason says magnanimously. "But watch yourself."

"I'm right here," I say to no one in particular.

Pretending not to hear, Levi does his job as if I were radioactive, and then he and Mason discuss who is to catch me if I need to be caught by the next tree. Surprise, surprise—that someone is going to be Mason.

"And who's going to catch Mason if he needs catching?" I ask.

"Trent." Levi points into the distance. "He's already in position."

Let's hope that Trent is old enough to have a learner's permit.

"Trent will not need to do anything." Mason sticks his chest out. "I can handle using a glove to brake."

I narrow my eyes at him. "Are you implying that I can't?"

"No," Levi and Mason say in unison.

"It's just a precaution," Levi adds.

"Because we don't want anyone to get hurt." Mason looks at Levi meaningfully.

I roll my eyes and watch as Mason leaps from the platform, making it look hella fun.

Except, I could swear I see someone catch him on the other end.

Huh.

So much for that confidence. Now it's more important than ever that I brake properly. That'll show him.

"Can you go already?" a male voice mutters from behind me.

I turn to see who the speaker is, but it seems he doesn't have a spine because everyone looks back at me blankly.

Whatever.

Bravely, I leap into the void.

Whoosh! I zip over faster than I can blink, screaming in glee, my adrenaline spiking higher than on any roller coaster.

A few feet from my destination, I remember the brake, but it's too late.

I don't even get the chance to touch the cable with my glove before I smash into a very familiar chest. One that smells tellingly masculine, with a hint of pines covered in snow.

"I've got you," Mason murmurs.

Why do I feel so gooey? It must be the aftereffects of the ride.

Also, as I was flying through the air, the straps further pushed on my groin, and Mason's proximity is making my blood rush into the area, which all conspires to create a strange sensation, almost like I might—

"Step over here," booms a voice that must belong to Trent.

Huh. Trent is huge and ancient. Maybe this is a family business, with Trent being Levi's grandpa?

Turns out, Mason doesn't discriminate against older males when it comes to the heavy-handed attempts to prevent me from their touches. He tells Trent exactly what he told his-maybe-grandson.

"Fine. Less work for me," Trent grumbles. "Now wait 'til everyone gathers."

"But you may clip her carabiner," Mason adds.

Trent just grunts.

The rest of the group takes turns smacking into Trent, except for Levi, who brakes expertly—raising my confidence in his abilities a notch or two.

Then Levi zips over to the next location, and Mason follows—and manages to brake in time.

All right.

I don't care if I have to ignore the fun aspect of this ride. I *have* to brake.

I leap.

Must brake.

The straps push even deeper into my bikini area, pushing the folds of my clothes against my other folds, creating a pressure on my clit that—

I smash into Mason once again… with a moan that I pray Levi will mistake for pain, but it's really pleasure.

An orgasm, to be precise.

Is this why the French call it "the little death"?

Because I might just die of mortification.

Chapter 25

Mason

Seems like when you get horny enough, wet dreams aren't sufficient and your brain starts to provide you with sexy hallucinations. When I catch Sophia in my arms, her expression looks just like her O-face—an image that is the most valuable possession stored in the safety box of my spank bank.

Speaking of said bank, I've made many deposits into it today: from the way the straps pushed up her boobs to—

"Can you let me go?" Sophia gasps.

Ah. Right. I gently separate us. "Are you okay?"

"Oh, yeah," she breathes. "That was... amazing." For some reason, she looks very flushed.

Levi clears his throat. "Can you please step aside so the rest can ride?"

Translation: "Get a room."

We move over. I'm barely walking because I'm hard and the fucking straps are painfully tight.

"Can I clip her in?" Levi asks cautiously when it's our turn again.

Fucking hell. Every time Levi reminds Sophia that I'm acting like a possessive boyfriend, her eyes narrow. If he keeps it up, she's going to give me a lecture... and probably have a point.

Yeah. When she refused to kiss me last night, she made it clear she's not "mine" in any sense of that word, but I just can't help myself. I can't stand the idea of another man touching her to the point where I don't even like knowing she's been with a guy in the past. In fact, some atavistic part of me was pleased when I learned that she's never had a serious relationship. If it were up to that part of me, Sophia would've remained a virgin until we met, like some Victorian debutante.

Ugh. Someone shoot me and put me out of my misery.

"Hey." Sophia elbows me in the chest. "Your turn."

Ah. Right. I jump from the platform—and can't help but grin. All the sexual tension aside, ziplining is great fun.

I manage to brake again and take my place to wait for an even more fun moment: when Sophia ends up in my embrace.

Fuck.

I'm anticipating this way too much, especially considering she doesn't want me like that. The last thing I need is to become an actual stalker.

Sophia zooms down super fast, except this time, she

brakes and lands gracefully in front of me on the platform like a ziplining pro.

"Great job." I can't help a wave of pride despite my disappointment that I didn't get to touch her.

She looks at me strangely. "Thank you, Mason."

Not sure what that was, but I like the sound of my name on her lips… especially when she screams it in pleasure.

And there we go again. My balls are beyond blue now. I think they're in violet territory. Maybe even ultraviolet. In fact, I wouldn't be surprised if they started shooting X-rays at all the Sophia-related X-rated images that swirl in my head.

XXX rays.

"Move over," Trent grumbles.

Ah. Right. We step aside to allow the other people to zip down, but the air between me and Sophia feels charged… or so my imagination makes me think.

"This is the last jump." She gestures at the wire we're about to ride. "Is it too early to say this excursion wasn't a clusterfuck?"

"No." At least my brain thinks so. My cock might consider this lack of a fuck a clusterfuck.

"Then why don't you tell me—"

"Move it," says some dude.

I glare over my shoulder, but no one takes credit for speaking, a smart move.

I turn back to face her. "Sorry, Ladybug. We'll have to continue this on the ground."

With that, I jump—and once again, a grin is on my face as the wind hits my cheeks.

They clearly saved the best for last.

This zip has the best zap.

In fact, I almost forget to brake, but the prospect of ending up in Levi's smells-like-teen-spirit embrace is a great motivator, so I do what's needed and land on the platform with just a slight misstep.

On her end, Sophia nails another perfect landing, which may be why I want to nail *her* all that much more.

"Spill it," she pants.

I shake my head. "We need to get to the ground. If either of us breaks an arm en route, this will be considered a clusterfuck after all."

She pouts but leaves me be until we're safely on the ground.

"Okay," she says. "Tell me now, or else."

I sigh. "Fine. Here goes. Remember when I told your friend Abigail that I could pass her resume on to someone at Octothorpe?"

Sophia's warm brown eyes widen to almost comical levels. "She's getting an interview?"

I nod. "Plus, I have it on good authority that her chances are solid."

What Landon actually said was: "Unless HR finds pictures of her shooting heroin into her eyeballs, or she shits on the desk of one of the interviewers, she's got the job in the bag," but I don't want to get Sophia's hopes too high in case Abigail finds a less spectacular way to screw up this opportunity.

"When is the interview?" Sophia demands.

"She had her first round yesterday," I say. "But she's got many more rounds to go."

Sophia's eyes go from wide to narrow. "You sat on something this big this whole time?"

"It was only an exclusive secret on the day we boarded," I say. "I wanted to use it to earn some goodwill so you'd stay for dinner. Abigail would've told you about it the next day if it weren't for your digital detox."

Now Sophia's eyes are just slits. "That's pretty manipulative."

I cock my head. "Would you rather I hadn't passed on her resume?"

"I'd rather you'd done it out of the goodness of your heart, not just to get something from me."

I arch an eyebrow. The truth is, I would've done it regardless, but if I tell her that now, she won't believe me anyway, or she'll call it another attempt at manipulation. For whatever reason, she thinks the worst of me, and I hate that.

"Okay, fine," she says curtly. "You win."

My other eyebrow shoots up. "Win what?"

My cock twitches—as if it's not clear what he's hoping she'll say.

"We can have dinner together when we get back on the ship," she says magnanimously.

I didn't ask for that, but I'm more than happy to

accept. "Sure. I'd love to have dinner with you tonight." And every dinner after that.

"Oh, and... thank you." Sophia steps closer to me and moistens her lips. "Whatever your motives, getting Abigail that interview was huge."

I can't drag my gaze away from her lips. "You're welcome."

She closes the distance between us. "Can you help me get out of this getup?"

I do as she requested, peeling off the harness straps one by one.

Fuck.

Who knew stripping off safety gear could be such a turn-on? Given how hard I am, you'd think these straps were lacy underwear.

"Let me help you too," she croons after I dumbly help her remove her helmet—like she couldn't do such a basic thing herself.

Help me?

Wait a—

Yep.

She drops to her knees, her mouth inches away from my throbbing cock. She frees my right leg, then my left—and it's a marvel I'm able to remain standing because I don't think there's any blood left anywhere but in my dick.

"Now your shoulders." Her voice is oddly sensual, probably due to my libido-driven hallucinations. "Sit."

I plant my ass on a nearby log, where she joins me and helps me undo the rest of the gear. She takes off my helmet last, and her face ends up a breath away from mine, her lips mere inches away.

Plump lips.

Juicy, temping lips that—

Suddenly, the lips I've been admiring so much lock with mine.

Fuck me. I have no idea if I initiated this, or she did. All I know is that it's the best kiss of my life—and most importantly, instead of pushing me away, she enthusiastically participates in the kiss.

"Just get a room." Trent glowers from somewhere nearby.

I suppress the urge to beat the old man into a bloody pulp. He's actually got a point.

Sophia and I in a room together is the best idea I've ever heard.

Chapter 26

Sophia

When I drag myself away from Mason, I see that everyone who was with us on the zipline —from too-young-to-see-this Levi to the maybe-grandfather—is staring at the two of us like we're masturbating chimps at the zoo.

I leap to my feet. "Let's go." If I'm lucky, I'll never see any of these people again.

Nodding, Mason stands up and leads me to our ride, his gait a little strange.

On the ride back and during dinner, we pretend that the scorching kiss didn't happen, which is good, because it probably shouldn't have happened, no matter how good it felt at the time. Instead, the conversation continues in the get-to-know-each-other vein, and I can't help but be greedy for every morsel of information he imparts, like the fact that he was recruited into hockey at the ripe old age of five. Nor can I resist it when he passionately talks about *Planet Earth*, his favorite nature documentary.

"I have a confession to make," he says when dessert is sadly over. "I arranged for a surprise for you tonight, but if you don't—"

"I want." Was that too forward?

"Good," he says. "What's your shoe size?"

I blink at him. I thought he was talking about Uber wrapped in a bow, but what would that have to do with my shoe size? Unless... does Mason have a foot fetish? He didn't seem to on F-Day, but that doesn't mean anything.

"Size eight." I hope that's small (or large?) enough to get him in the right mood.

"Thanks." He texts someone one digit, and I can only assume it's the number eight.

Okay. There's every possibility that the surprise isn't happening in Mason's bedroom.

My overzealous curiosity engaged, I follow him through the ship and into the elevator, which takes us to deck three.

Hmm. I vaguely recall a mention of some cool attraction on this deck. But I can't—

A cool breeze and a sign reading "Ice Rink" clue me in just as my memory was about to.

"We're going ice skating?" I say, not bothering to hide the excitement in my voice.

"I should've blindfolded you," Mason says grumpily.

Yes. That would have been pretty hot.

He opens the large doors in front of us, exposing a

giant room covered in ice. "As you have guessed, the surprise is that we're going skating."

I drag my mind out of the gutter. "I don't know how to skate." Is that why my heart is hammering so wildly?

Mason grins. "I figured, which is why I plan to teach you."

"Teach me?" I take a tentative step toward the ice. For whatever reason, I find the idea of him teaching as fascinating as the blindfold.

"Don't worry," he says. "I've got you."

I swallow, my throat peculiarly dry. "Okay."

Summoning my courage, I step into the chilly room and see a bunch of gear Mason must've had someone prepare for us. There are two pairs of skates, one helmet, one pair of gloves, thick snow pants, and elbow and knee pads. Last but not least, there's a gizmo that looks like a walker an elderly person might use after hip replacement surgery.

I wrinkle my nose at the safety gear. "You really didn't have much confidence in my skating skills, huh?"

Mason effortlessly slips on his skates. "I don't want you to hurt yourself." He picks up the smaller skates. "Now, let's put these on."

I put on the snow pants first because I doubt I can get inside them with skates, then sit on the bench and give Mason my feet as per his demand. Given the gentle care with which he puts on those skates, the foot fetish idea resurfaces, except it seems like I'm the one who has it because I very much like it when his strong fingers brush over my arches.

He then fits a helmet onto my head for the second time today—and I almost kiss him again. However, when it comes to the knee and elbow pads, I insist on dealing with them myself, mostly because I don't think I can control myself for much longer—and we are in public, even if there's nobody around.

"Perfect." He looks me over approvingly. "Let's start with you just standing, getting comfortable with the skates."

I step onto the rink and do as he says, even though the way he's holding my hand makes my brain turn to mush—and that's despite the gloves.

Once I'm more or less adjusted to the feeling of the skates, he brings over the walker thing, and I use it to wobble around a bit, getting more comfortable by the minute.

"I think I can go without it," I say after some time.

"Okay." He glides over to me with the grace of a figure skater. "Hold my hand."

I push the walker away and grip his hand for all I'm worth. We begin to move over the ice, and it feels surreally like dancing, especially when he takes both of my hands in his and twirls me in a circle.

"Let me try this on my own," I say after a few more minutes.

"I'm not sure you're ready," he says.

Should I tell him that his touch is too intoxicating, and that I might actually be safer on my own? No. Instead, I just give him my best puppy eyes. "I can do it. Please."

He gingerly lets go of my hands. "Go slow. Be careful."

"Of course," I say... and then, in an eyeblink, without any warning, I faceplant right onto the ice.

Whoosh. Thanks to all the padding, all I feel is the wind getting knocked out of me. Then strong arms pick me up, and I feel myself getting carried somewhere.

By the time I recover my wits, we're in the elevator, with me clasped securely against Mason's chest.

"Where are we going?" I mumble.

"My room," he says. "I've got some first aid there. You scratched your chin."

Huh. My chin does feel a bit sore. But hey, aside from that, I don't feel any pain whatsoever, though I'm not sure if that's because I didn't really get hurt or because of all the endorphins flooding my body thanks to his touch.

The elevator stops, and Mason takes long strides toward his destination.

Once we're in his suite, Mason takes me to the giant bed and drapes me over it, looking at my chin like a heart surgeon might peer into an open chest cavity.

"How do you feel?" he asks.

So turned on that I could come, but I can't tell him *that*. "There's no pain," I say. "I felt some soreness at first, but even that's gone." Or deafened by the tsunami-sized spikes of hormones.

"I will disinfect it," he says. "Can I leave you alone for a second?"

"Like I said, I'm fine." Hell, I want some soreness... just not on my chin.

He leaves me reluctantly, as though he's worried that I'm putting on a brave face and might still break into tiny shards as soon as I'm out of his view. When he's finally gone, I rush to rid myself of the bulky, dorky gear, starting with the elbow pads and working my way down. I also fix my hair as much as the nearby mirror allows—and then I wonder how fun it would be to see him fucking me in this mirror, which is clearly here for that explicit purpose.

I blush at the thought, and this is when he comes back, of course. Walking up to me, he sits on the bed and gently lifts my chin with his finger.

Oh, boy.

He dabs the imaginary boo-boo with an alcohol swab and tenderly blows on my chin.

By Odin's beard, his lips are too temptingly puckered and too near me. Unable to help myself, I lean toward them, like a slutty moth toward a cock-shaped flame.

Mason's breath catches as he realizes what I'm doing. Leaning in as well, he meets me with a kiss that starts off gentle but quickly turns anything but. Our tongues tangle, and the kiss begins to remind me of his hockey game: fierce, bold, and hot.

I'm panting, my head spinning, when he somehow manages to pull back.

"You okay?" he asks, his voice low and rough.

"I want my skates off." Or else the headlines might

read: "Owner chops off arm of best player on team while canoodling with him."

He nods, and his face develops a look of tough concentration, like he's exerting a great deal of control over his baser instincts. He removes my footwear, followed by my socks. And then, as though he's developed psychic powers, he begins to massage my feet, starting with the arch and moving over to each toe, his hot breath making it feel like he's licking them too—or maybe he is. I'm too blissed out to be sure.

So yeah, I am definitely into foot stuff, and maybe he is as well. No matter how turned on I thought I was before, it was nothing compared to how I feel now. I want to strip him naked and have his lips suck Plato and Socrates's nipples. I want him to fill me with his—

In another psychic moment, Mason begins to strip for me.

"Yes," I gasp. "Take it all off."

I clearly made that too vague. I meant for *him* to be naked, but he strips *me* instead—and only after that does he unleash Uber.

"Are we doing this?" His words are almost guttural, and I again get the feeling that pausing to ask questions is costing him a great deal of self-control.

On his end, Uber seems to wink cockily at me, like he's saying, "We all know you want me."

I dampen my lips. "Do you know the Sin City slogan?"

Mason stares at me like a wolf at a newborn rabbit. "What happens in Vegas stays in Vegas?"

I scooch toward him on the bed. "This cruise is our Vegas."

His gaze turns hooded. "Your eyes remind me of warm chocolate. Have I ever told you that?"

"You're not looking at my eyes." I circle my finger around my tight nipple—which is the current focus of his gaze. "Also, I thought you didn't eat chocolate. That when you crave something like that, you actually want fruit."

"You forget," he growls. "I eat lots of dark chocolate. You even thought it was obscene that I put it in my salads."

"Ah, right." I totally forgot. But in my defense, I'm face to tip with Uber, so my brain is running on estrogen fumes. "I guess I accept your compliment." Even if it makes me think of tossing a salad—the sex act, that is.

"Speaking of delicious things that I want to eat, lie back," he orders gruffly.

Oh, my.

I do as I am told, and he traces a path over my body with his tongue, starting with my right foot, over my calf and knee, and all the way up to where I'm quivering with need.

He feather-kisses my folds first, sending a shiver of pleasure through my every nerve ending. Then his kisses get deeper and fiercer, making me moan.

"Delicious," he breathes right into my flesh. Then he takes a luxurious lick over my clit, followed by another one, and another and another until an agonizingly sweet pressure coils in my core, leaving me panting and twisting in desperation.

"That's right," he grunts. "Come for me."

And do I ever. White specks dance in my vision, and my well-massaged toes curl spasmodically as I come all over his clever tongue.

"Good job," he murmurs before he slides his tongue down, passing by my perineum, and then, in yet another feat of psychic powers, he gives me a lick where the sun never shines.

A shudder ripples over my body, and I flush all over. This is embarrassing in a weirdly hot way. It feels tickly but good, especially when he squeezes my butt cheeks and orders me to relax.

Relax? How can I when he's sucking on his finger and then pressing that finger against the tight opening of my ass? Slowly, it slips inside, and the sensation is intense, the stretch a little painful—but again, in a weirdly sensual way.

Stranger still, when the finger is gone, I kind of miss it.

"Now," he rasps. "I want you from behind."

Oh. I'm pretty sure he means my pussy. Either way... "I thought you'd never ask." Limbs a little wobbly, I get on all fours and watch in the mirror as he positions himself behind me, Uber harder and thicker than I've ever seen it.

"Careful," I gasp as I watch him put on a condom. "You're too big."

"Of course," he says soothingly, and then he enters

me (yes, my pussy) slowly and gently, letting my muscles adjust as he goes. In the mirror, his face looks tormented, like it's taking a herculean effort of will to exude such control. Then, almost teasingly, he pulls Uber out.

No. I want—

He slowly glides back in, and it goes in as smoothly as a panna cotta does into my mouth, thanks to the copious moisture I'm producing.

"Faster," I shock myself by saying. "Harder. Deeper."

Grunting something unintelligible, he delivers on my demands, thrusting into me like a man possessed.

My moans grow in pitch and desperation.

"Come," he orders just as I'm doing so anyway.

With a scream, I clench around Uber, and barely remain on all fours afterward.

"Give me another one," he grunts greedily.

Staying on all fours is the best I can do as far as replies go, but he helps me with that anyway by grabbing on to Socrates before thrusting into me with renewed vigor.

My eyes roll back into my head. A new orgasm builds in my core, but it seems far away, almost out of—

His finger returns to where it was in my ass, creating an overwhelming sensation that gives me an explosive burst of pleasure—one that leaves me almost hoarse from all the moans and screams.

"One more time," he growls. "You can do it."

If I could speak, I'd tell him that I don't share his

confidence—but then I feel him let go of Socrates and grab a handful of my hair.

Oh, fuck. Realizing my eyes are closed, I open them and stare at the mirror.

Yes! He's grasping my hair in a hard, veiny, premium fist, and the sight of it is like applying a powerful vibrator right up to my oversensitive clit.

I come, screaming his name.

As I squeeze around Uber for the last time, Mason grunts in pleasure, and I feel his release, which makes me spasm again in a weak aftershock.

Panting, I fall into a heap on the bed, unable to move a single muscle. Faintly, I'm aware of Mason cleaning me up and then wrapping himself around me like a billion-dollar blanket.

"Nice," I mutter.

He snorts. "Just nice?"

"Oh, the sex was divine." I yawn. "I meant the spooning is nice."

"Ah." He kisses the nape of my neck. "I was about to demand a rematch."

"That we can discuss tomorrow," I say over another yawn. "So long as you remember that 'what happens on the cruise...'"

"'...stays on the cruise,'" he says, his tone hard to decipher.

"That's right." I cozy backward into him. "Now I'm going to sleep."

And just like that, I'm out.

Chapter 27

Mason

This is how I want to wake up from now on—with Sophia in my arms.

What happens on the cruise stays on the cruise.

Not fucking likely. Not if I have anything to say about it.

I draw her closer.

It's official. My new mission is: make sure this thing between us—whatever it is—continues after the cruise.

I just need a strategy, like I would in a game.

Yeah. For starters, no more talk about buying the team. Instead, I can offer to help her run it... though she might get offended by that. Maybe instead, I could—

"Morning." She opens one eye. "Did I snore?"

"No." I smile at her sleepy face. "You were quiet, like a hibernating ladybug."

She opens both eyes. "They hibernate?"

"In the winter. They don't eat while they hibernate, but if the weather gets extra cold, they might come out for a snack."

"A great idea." She wriggles out of my embrace and sits up before sliding her feet off the bed. "I'm starving."

Deliciously naked, she beelines for the bathroom. I take a moment to calm my instantly-at-attention dick, and then I make a call to make sure her shoes and our other items are returned from the ice rink.

When she comes out of the bathroom, sadly wrapped in a robe, I'm not surprised to learn that she wants to swing by her own suite.

"Your shoes will be outside the door," I tell her.

She darts a glance at her bare feet. "Ah. Right. Thanks."

I wave the thanks away. "Which restaurant are we getting breakfast at?"

"The usual," she says, not questioning the "we" part. "I'm dying to know more facts about ladybugs."

I'm not sure if she is kidding or not, but once we meet up, I tell her what I can remember from the beetle documentary I watched. Fascinating factoids such as: ladybugs bleed from their knees when threatened, and their larva look like micro gators, and they have claws that help them sit on surfaces, and the creepiest fact of all—they lay extra eggs as a snack for their young.

"Oh, and they have an adorable collective noun," I say in conclusion.

"They do?"

"Yeah. A group of them is called a loveliness of ladybugs." Which is fitting, considering how lovely the ladybug in front of me is.

"And that's all?" she asks.

"Yeah."

Sophia narrows her eyes. "How come you didn't tell me that they taste bad? Or that their coloring is a warning of that fact? Those are the only things I knew about ladybugs before today."

I shrug. "I've only tasted one ladybug thus far, and she was delicious."

Predictably, her face reddens to a shade not that different from a ladybug's bright hue. I guess it might be too much to tell her another truth: regardless of her coloring, she need not worry about predators ever again—not while I'm still breathing.

She slurps her macchiato. "So... what are we doing today?"

"How about we try the surfing simulator after this?" I offer, keeping a poker face to hide the fact that her "we" makes me want to pump my fist in the air.

She cocks her head. "You surf?"

"No, but I'm a quick learner."

———

Turns out, Sophia is a much quicker learner than I am —at least if we go by the number of times each of us wipes out on the simulator. In my defense, half of my falls happened because I got distracted by staring at her in her bathing suit.

"You ice skate so well I thought you'd be good at balancing activities in general," she says while we're waiting in line to ride again.

She's referring to the somersault I accidentally performed during wipeout number fifty-seven.

"I'm sure I could master surfing if I wanted to," I say with a confidence I don't quite feel.

She shakes her head. "I'd stick with hockey if I were you. It's what you're good at."

I lean in to whisper into her ear, "Are you sure you can't think of something else that I'm good at?"

Just as I intended, Sophia blushes once again.

———

For the next few days, we're inseparable. Together, we go cage-diving with sharks, take history tours, ride an electric tram, and go snorkeling. During meals and when commuting to those excursions, we learn more about one another—and no matter how much I learn about her, it's never enough.

Of course, the highlight of each day happens in my suite, where we thoroughly explore each other's bodies, learning what the other likes and dislikes. Oh, and I'm not keeping score or anything, but I'm positive that I've made Sophia come three times for each of my orgasms.

When we reach Jamaica, we nearly break our necks

climbing a six-hundred-foot waterfall. Afterward, one of the tour guides offers to sell us some weed.

"Can we?" Sophia looks at me pleadingly.

"Why?" I narrow my eyes at the guide. "We can't take it on the ship."

The guide grins her overly toothy smile. "I could just sell you a couple of joints that you can smoke before you head back."

I frown. "I don't do drugs."

"We've already had this conversation," Sophia says. "You drink, and alcohol is a drug."

"How about just one joint?" the guide suggests.

Sophia fishes out a soaking-wet bill from her pocket. "Will this cover it?"

Eyes shining with avarice, the guide snatches the bill away before I can see what denomination it is. "This will do," she says. "And—for my new favorite customer—here's a bonus." She pulls a cheap plastic lighter out of her purse and gives it to Sophia along with the joint. "I'd recommend you go smoke it over there." She points to a spot near the water. "The view is nice, and I'll make sure no one bothers you."

Sophia elbows me challengingly. "Will you go with me, or are you too afraid of contact high?"

"I'll go," I say. "But that doesn't mean I approve of this."

"Noted," Sophia says, and under her breath, she mutters something that sounds like "narc."

When we get to the secluded corner, I have to admit that the view here *is* nice... at least until Sophia lights up her joint and blows out a cloud of smoke that obscures said view.

"Doesn't that destroy brain cells?" I ask her.

She coughs. "Alcohol does as well. Now can you please stop being a buzzkill?"

I sigh. Weirdly, the drug smells kind of nice. Very herbal, which makes sense, but also earthy and with hints of either lemon or apple, though that might well be Sophia's shampoo. Also, the way her lips wrap around that—

"Is this what peer pressure is like?" I grumble out loud. Because a part of me wants to try the stupid thing. Though she's much too young to be a peer.

She was in kindergarten when I was under actual peer pressure in high school.

She arches an eyebrow. "Does that mean you want to have a puff? I assure you, the addiction potential is—"

"Let me guess, 'less than that of alcohol,'" I say.

She nods.

"Fine." I extend my hand. "Give it."

I take the joint, suck in some smoke, and let it out.

She narrows her eyes. "You didn't inhale."

I frown. "I didn't?"

She cocks her head. "You've never smoked anything before?"

"No. I'm a fucking athlete. Why would I?"

She snatches the joint back. "Do this." She drags in such a big lungful of air that her stomach expands.

"Got it." I take the joint back and do as she

suggested… and begin coughing like I have tuberculosis, bronchitis, and pneumonia all at once.

"That was too much," Sophia says when I can breathe again. "Do it more like this." She takes the joint, and her ample bosom rises and falls, making my dick hard once again.

When she hands me the joint, I inhale slower and gentler, but I cough once again.

"Have you ever meditated?" she demands.

I nod.

"Breathe in like that." As she demonstrates, her boobs bob up and down once more, sending the rest of my blood into my already-throbbing cock.

I do a meditative inhale, but the coughing fit that follows is even worse.

She rolls her eyes. "How about I shotgun you?"

"You what me?"

"It's when I exhale the smoke into your mouth while you inhale." She takes in a drag and rises on tiptoes, like we're about to kiss.

Fuck me.

Our lips lock, and she does what she described. As I inhale her smoke-laced breath, I realize that her statement about weed's lack of addictiveness is bullshit.

If it were delivered this way all the time, I'd be a pothead forever.

"Again?" she asks after she pulls away.

I nod.

She does the shotgun thing, again and again, until the joint is gone… which is when I realize that an invisible purple sausage is flying around my head and singing "Happy Birthday" in Estonian.

Wait, what?

That doesn't make sense.

Today isn't my birthday.

Whoa. Mason's eyes turn bloodshot and watery, and his pupils dilate.

Huh.

"You know what would happen if you were a teacher who overfed his students fried sticks of butter?" I ask.

"They wouldn't eat the flying sausages?" Mason gestures at empty air.

"No." But a smoked sausage sounds really good. "Your pupils would dilate."

Hmm. Fried sticks of butter also sound delicious all of a sudden.

Ah. Right. Despite my high tolerance, I'm high as a kite made out of cannabis.

Ha-ha. My high is high. That's hilarious.

"I want to go swimming with dolphins," Mason says, eyes gleaming with excitement. "Or manatees. Or giraffes."

I grin. Even when his brain is jumbled by THC, he wants a nature show. "Let's see if we can make one of those happen." I grab his hand and lead him away.

I'm not sure if it's the pot or the rough, callused texture of his palm, but my sex drive goes into overdrive by the time we find ourselves in a cab.

Sex drive into overdrive. I'm on a roll.

I giggle out loud.

It seems that Mason isn't immune to my touch either, because in response to my giggle, he gives me the kiss of my life, one that lasts forever.

Panting, we pull apart as the cab comes to a stop in front of the dolphin joint.

Oh. A dolphin *joint*.

I snort-laugh at my own wittiness.

Mason is oblivious. Staring at my lips, he asks huskily, "Can we get some *taranka*?"

I blink at him. "Tarantula?"

There's no way I'm swimming with one of those. Or kissing one.

Come to think of it, I wouldn't even smoke a joint with one.

Mason frowns. "Tarantula? They're not salty."

I'm growing concerned. "Salty?"

"*Taranka*," he says. "It's a species of roach."

I shudder. "That's even worse."

He cocks his head. "It is? You catch them, salt them, and let them air dry. They're the best beer snack."

I almost throw up. "Cockroaches as snacks?"

Maybe Mason was right not to want to smoke weed with me. There're munchies, and then there's this.

"Roach," Mason says again. "It's a type of fish. *Rutilus heckelii*."

Oh. "You want fish jerky?"

He nods.

That doesn't sound like a bad idea. "Let's check that store."

I lead him into a shop, but the closest thing we find to what he craves is something called *Jamaican Jerk*, a brand of potato chips.

Then again, who knew potatoes could be such a good replacement for a roach... I mean, a fish. Mason devours his bag with such enthusiasm that I feel a little jealous. But then when I bite into my chosen snack— tamarind balls—I forget where I am because they're so good.

We consume everything we bought and return to raid the store for more.

After a few more snack trips, I manage to recall what we're here for and drag Mason over to the seaquarium.

As we gear up, I get to enjoy the sight of Mason's naked torso, but then, sadly, he covers it with a flotation device. Soon, we're in the water and face to face with a pod of dolphins.

My heartbeat speeds up as a look of childlike wonder comes over Mason's face, and for some strange reason, I picture a little boy with my and Mason's features wearing that exact expression.

No. Hold up. That's insane, and a great reason to say no to drugs from here on out.

"You really can?" Mason says to the more smiley of the dolphins.

"He can what?" I ask.

Mason turns my way. "Flop, here, can read my thoughts." Turning back to his new friend, he adds, "And I his."

Wow. Can he really?

No. That's the weed talking... I think.

Flop gives me a squinty stare and chirps, as if to say, "Bitch, you doubt my mighty powers?"

"Kiss his nose," the excursion guide tells Mason. "And I'll take a picture."

Mason reverently kisses Flop—if that really is his name—and I feel the greenest jealousy of my life.

Flop chirps excitedly, the smiling bastard.

"Now *you* go," the guide tells me.

I point at a different dolphin. "Can I kiss her?"

"That's a him," the guide says. "But go for it."

"No," Mason states. "The only male she can kiss is me."

With an eyeroll, I ask which dolphin is female and give that one a peck on her wet, rubbery nose for the camera.

"How was that?" I ask Mason sarcastically. "Did you feel like you were watching two girls making out?"

Mason seems too preoccupied with his telepathic connection to Flop, so he doesn't answer for a minute or so. Then he snarls, "No, Flop, you can't eat my cat."

Flop chirps something excitedly.

Mason's hand makes a fist, which makes my nether regions flutter. "If you so much as mention my cat again," the owner of the fist growls, "I'll wipe that smug smile off your face with your gills. And yes, I know you don't have gills."

"And that is our cue to get going." I grab a hold of Mason's flotation device and drag him to the pool steps —before proper authorities get involved.

When we get into the cab, Mason looks around with a worried expression. "How come everyone knows I did drugs?"

Should I tell him that talking to dolphins could be a tiny clue? "You're just being paranoid," I say instead.

"No," he says. "*They* know."

The way he says *they* makes me think of conspiracy theorists.

All right. I've got to help Mason. Somehow.

I frantically look around before settling on a possible solution.

"Sir," I say to the driver. "Can I borrow those?" I point at the headphones lying on the dashboard.

"Five dollars, and they're yours," the driver says.

I pay the enterprising cabby his fee before putting the headphones over Mason's ears. Connecting them to his phone, I unleash Pink Floyd on said ears.

As expected, Mason's features relax, settling into a blissed-out expression.

Midway into the ride, without opening his eyes, he says, "I'm having such a great time with you."

Me? Pink Floyd? Or did he reestablish his telepathic connection to Flop?

Either way, the words make a loveliness of ladybugs flap their wings in my belly. "I'm also having a great time with you," I confess.

"Good," he says, eyes still closed. "There's something else I've been meaning to tell you."

"What?" And again, I hope he is talking to me.

"I love you," Mason says with a smile.

The shock is such that the ladybugs in my belly choke on their tongues. "What did you just say?"

And to whom?

Mason doesn't answer.

He's fallen into a drug-induced sleep.

Chapter 29

Mason

Stupid. Stupid. Stupid.

I'm never doing drugs again.

How could I have told Sophia that I love her before I'm even sure of that?

What's worse, I know she isn't on the same page. Or the same book. Or the same library.

To let the issue die, I fake sleep, which isn't hard, as "Comfortably Numb" is playing in my ears.

Suddenly, I have a great idea.

Genius level, I'm sure.

Maybe I should write it down?

No. It's so good I'll remember it later, for sure.

It has to do with books, which are on my mind for some unknown reason. A novel idea, to be precise. A retelling of Pinocchio, but instead of his nose growing, it will be his cock. And not when he's lying, but when he—

No, wait. How old is Pinocchio? Better make him a

consenting adult.

Yeah. But hold on. I've been having trouble with excessive erections as of late, and now I'm writing about a guy with the same issue. Is this idea too on the nose... or cock?

Maybe I should make this Pinocchio female?

But what part of her would grow? Her clit? And under what circumstances?

The car stops.

"Mason?" Sophia whispers.

I pretend to wake up, and we board the ship—where, despite what Sophia says, I'm convinced that everyone knows I'm stoned.

Huh. Stoned. That could easily be the term for a hard-on, which I have at the moment, thanks to Sophia's proximity.

Maybe I'm Pinocchio? Or Pinocchia? No, wait, I'm not a girl. And it's definitely my cock that's growing.

"You know what I'm in the mood for?" Sophia asks.

I lean in and nibble her ear. "A hard fuck?"

Her pupils—the eye kind, not the student kind—dilate. "I was going to say visiting the all-you-can-eat buffet," she says huskily. "But... I like your idea a lot better."

I press the elevator button for the suite deck. "Luckily for me, I'll still get something delicious to eat."

Her reply is a kiss that lasts until we're in the suite.

"Hey," she says breathlessly. "How did we get here without unlocking our lips?"

I stare at her and ponder the same mystery. "I have no idea. Maybe some sexy crab-walking was involved?"

She snorts. "Nothing about crabs is sexy."

My nostrils flare. "The Russian equivalent of doggy style is crayfish."

"Not the same crustaceans." She starts to strip. "I do like where your mind is at, though."

As soon as her smooth skin is exposed, I cover it with kisses—that is, until she takes her shoes off.

Dropping to my knees, I give her a foot rub just the way she likes, then nibble on her toes until her breathing turns shallow and her pussy glistens too invitingly for me to ignore.

"The buffet is open for business," I mutter, grabbing her hips.

Her skin reddens all over.

Leaning in, I taste her as I've wanted to do all day and find that somehow, unbelievably, she's even sweeter and silkier than I recall.

"Yes, just like that," she moans as I suck on her clit.

Inhaling the intoxicating scent of her sex, I keep a steady pace until she comes all over my mouth. Only then do I pull away to look up at her flushed face.

"That's a good start," I say huskily and pick her up to lay her on the bed. "But you owe me a few more of those."

She licks her lips, staring up at me as I get on top of her. Her voice is breathless as I begin nibbling my way down her collarbone to her chest. "A burden, to be sure. But first, I have a craving for Uber."

I stop midway to her nipple and lift my head to pin her with a confused stare. "Do you mean Uber Eats?"

She bites her lip. "I nicknamed your cock Uber."

Huh. "You did?"

"It has to do with Nietzsche," she says. "Not any sort of ride sharing." She narrows her eyes at my cock. "I don't want to share him with anyone."

Fair enough.

I point at her pussy. "I don't want to share Lyft either."

"Lift? Like British for elevator? Is it because you're thinking about riding... up and down?"

"No, Lyft with a 'Y,' like the app. But yes, I want Lyft riding Uber all night long."

She bites her lip. "That can be arranged." She points at her right breast. "Since we're on the subject of names, this is Plato." She points at the other side. "And this is Socrates."

I arch an eyebrow. "In that case, I'd like to cup Socrates and Plato." I match actions to my words. "Next, I'm going to suck Socrates and Plato's nipples." I do this too until she moans.

"Not fair," she gasps. "I still haven't gotten my fill of Uber."

Oh. Right.

I pull away and lie on my back, Uber jutting out like a mast on a ship chock full of horny pirates.

Sophia takes me into her mouth, making my head spin.

"Fuck, Ladybug… That feels so good, we should name your mouth… or tongue."

Her reply is a flick of said tongue around Uber's head.

"Ayn Rand?" I suggest gutturally.

Sophia looks up at me, cock still in her wet, silky mouth, an as-yet-unnamed-eyebrow raised.

"She was a philosopher as well as a novelist," I somehow manage to explain. "With her being Russian-American, I—"

Sophia takes Uber deeper until I feel her throat, and further conversation becomes impossible. Thinking too. Hell, I'm lucky I remember how to breathe—but even there, I'm barely succeeding. My inhales are shallow and fast, exhales loud and bordering on groans of pleasure.

"Stop," I manage to grunt when she ice-cream licks the head. "I want to be inside you."

Without my prompting, she sheaths Uber with a condom and gets on all fours.

Such a good girl.

"Fucking hot," I whisper into her ear as I enter her.

I move slowly at first, but then she arches her back and demands I speed up, and I'm all too happy to oblige.

"Yes!" she screams as she spasms around me.

"Next time, scream my name." I grab a handful of her hair—something that I've noticed seems to drive her crazy.

"Just fuck me," she moans, her gaze on the mirror that reflects my fist in her hair. "Please!"

I love it when she begs for it. Beast-mode activated, I piston into her with everything I've got.

"Yes!" she cries. "Yes! Mason—"

She comes so hard her tight walls squeeze Uber to the point where I can't take it anymore. Grunting her name, I burst inside her with an orgasm so intense my vision blurs.

It takes us both a long minute to recover. Finally, I find the strength to get up, so I can clean us up. Afterward, I lie next to her and gather her into a hug against me.

"That was nice," she murmurs sleepily. "And much better than an all-you-can-eat buffet."

I don't reply because I have a sudden dumb urge to tell her again that I love her. But I don't. I'm a tiny bit less stoned, and I've learned my lesson.

Unless she acknowledges that she heard me and hints that the feeling is mutual, I'm going to keep quiet and simply do everything in my power to make her fall for me.

I'll do whatever it takes.

"See," I say to Mason as we brush our teeth together the next morning. "The nice thing about pot is the lack of hangover the next day."

"I'm not so sure I agree." He checks his still-slightly-bloodshot eyes in the mirror. "I'm craving a bagel with cream cheese and lox. I've never craved that in my life. I blame the drugs."

Hmm. He was also craving salty fish yesterday. "It's possible it's not completely out of your system."

Who knew a two-hundred-pound hockey player would have such a low tolerance? I mean, he was so stoned that he told me he loved me. Or rather, he told someone—probably some unnamed salty fish. Or maybe he meant to send a telepathic message to Flop the Dolphin. Either way, he didn't mean it, I'm sure. It was just euphoria talking.

Hell, when I tried molly, I confessed my undying love to my new iPhone, so there's that.

But what if he did mean it, if only on some subconscious level?

Could it be that he at least likes me?

No. I can't go there. We agreed. What happens on the cruise stays on the cruise.

Besides, our fling, or whatever this is, is most likely about the team. As soon as we get back to NYC, he'll go back to trying to get me to sell.

Ugh. Should I sell it to him? Given how our first meeting unfolded, I was dead set against it, but I can no longer hold onto my spite.

This is important to him. So important he's pursued me into the open ocean. And he's right: what do I know about running a team, even with Abigail's help? But if I sell, will he disappear? Will the transaction sever whatever connection there is between us? Or will it—

"Ready?" he asks.

Shit. I've been standing here, staring dumbly into the mirror.

With effort, I shake off my funk. "Yeah. Let's go."

———

It's official. Mason is still stoned—how else to explain the fact that he just ate an actual doughnut?

Weirdly, I ate a piece of fruit myself.

"Seems like we've rubbed off on each other," he says with a grin when I point this out.

Yeah, we have, and we rub against each other some more that evening, and the evening after that. In general, we spend all our time together over the next couple of days—and they're the best days of my life.

After the doughnut breakfast, he gets the captain to give us a private tour of the ship, including areas that "no one has ever seen, or will see again... until two days from now."

"What happens two days from now?" I can't help but ask.

The captain takes a big gulp of vodka straight from the bottle. "Florida Bears are taking this very cruise," he explains excitedly. "Which means I get to meet my other favorite hockey player: Michael Medvedev."

Mason's expression darkens. "Don't tell him you're a fan of mine, or he might just punch you in the face."

"Oh." The captain chugs another liver-destroying dose of alcohol. "Thanks for the warning."

When the tour is over, I ask Mason about this Michael Medvedev, as it seems there's history there.

Mason's jaw tightens. "Misha is a rude fucker who thinks he's my equal, except he's not."

"Misha?" I blink in confusion.

"In Russian, that's a diminutive version of Michael, but it's also associated with bears. He hates it when people call him that, which is why I use it whenever I can."

"I see." When I think bears, I think Winnie the Pooh, Paddington, and Viking berserkers, but hey, whatever tickles your pet bear.

"Anyway," Mason continues, "he's got some talent, I'll give him that, but no ability as a team player. The

Yetis kicked him out after his first week, and he blames me for it, even though it was actually our coach who made that call. The only team that would take him after that were the Florida Bears, and they're at the bottom of the DHL barrel. But hey, I guess he's still famous enough to be on the captain's radar."

I wink at him. "The good captain does seem to have great taste when it comes to hockey players."

I'm not sure what exactly was seductive about that sentence, but Mason picks me up and carries me into his suite, where he gives me a full-body massage and fucks my brains out. Afterward, he surprises me with a romantic dinner for two on his balcony, which is followed by another divine-level fucking.

The next day, I learn that Mason has booked us a morning at the spa, as well as a private cabana to chillax in—and canoodle in. The day after that, he reserves a private outdoor hot tub surrounded by ocean views. And if that weren't romantic enough, he sets up a hammock on the very top deck of the ship so we can sleep under the stars.

Throughout all this pampering, I get the feeling like he's on the verge of asking me something, but he never does. I suspect he wants to ask me to sell the team, and I'm glad he doesn't voice that out loud because I want to pretend that he's with me for me. Plus I still haven't decided if I'll sell or not.

Or maybe I have decided. Selling is the only way to ensure that "what happens on the cruise stays on the cruise." Otherwise, he'll continue stalking me, and it would be all too easy to believe that it's not just my team he's after—and I can't allow myself to fall into that kind of trap again.

After Mom and Rupert, I would be an idiot to trust someone who I know has ulterior motives.

Still, even though I know that whatever is between Mason and me is an illusion, I find myself increasingly down as the end of the cruise nears... even as I continue to enjoy myself in Mason's company.

In fact, if it weren't for his company, I might get downright depressed.

On the night before our arrival back at Port Canaveral, I can no longer stave off the mopiness. Even the five orgasms he's given me this evening haven't helped. I am beyond depressed that the cruise is ending —and I feel dumb for feeling this way.

I knew this would end.

Knew that a joy such as I've experienced wouldn't last.

Not for me.

Never for me.

My chest tightens as I picture my life back in NYC. It's a good life—I have money, I have Abigail, I have my philosophy studies. I even have horny turtles... I mean, tortoises. Yet I feel hollow as I imagine going back to all that sans Mason.

In the past few days, he's stalked his way not just onto my cruise but also—

Mason turns over in his sleep, removing his arm from my shoulder.

I instantly feel cold.

I pull a blanket over myself, but it doesn't help. I can't sleep. The separation is looming over me like the sword of Damocles. Tossing and turning, I try to come up with a way to proceed that would not hurt... or would hurt the least.

Midway through the night, I decide I need to just rip off the Band-Aid. Or the full-body burn bandage, as it may be. I need to avoid any kind of emotional (possibly fake on his end) goodbyes and sneak out of his room and off the cruise before he wakes up. Once home, I'll get in touch with my lawyer and sell the team.

Yeah. Maybe if he calls me after that and still wants to see me—

No, I need to stop thinking in that direction. That way lies hope, and hope leads to heartbreak, as I've learned one too many times.

Still, a part of me wants to at least take a cab to the airport together. Or have breakfast. Or a goodbye fuck. But no. If we take that cab together, we'll be on land together, and he'll probably give me a dozen orgasms right there in front of the driver—and that'll be it. What happened on the cruise will have happened outside of the cruise... and I don't think I could bear it.

Not if it's meant to end, which, of course, it is.

Yet, even after the decision is made, I can't sleep a wink, not even when he rolls back and gathers me against him, teddy-bear style.

Especially not then.

After what feels like a week, the dawn finally arrives.

I carefully extricate myself from Mason's embrace. As I do so, the first rays of the rising sun illuminate Mason's chiseled features, making something in my chest flutter like the wings of a huge loveliness of ladybugs.

Am I making a mistake? What if he does want me for me? Or will, once he gets the team?

No. That's just hormones talking. The more important question is: what if he doesn't?

I'm too scared to find out.

Moving like a ninja, I sneak out of Mason's suite and into my own to get my stuff before sprinting for the VIP elevator.

The whole way down, a weak part of me hopes that Mason has woken up and decided to intercept me... but that's not the case.

I'm the first person to get in line for the exit, though a crowd piles up behind me pretty quickly.

Mason isn't among them.

When we dock, I escape from the ship and push my way through the people waiting to depart in the terminal. Among them are a bunch of huge dudes who must be the Florida Bears hockey team the captain mentioned the other day. How else to explain the broken noses and fierce expressions?

It's not like Vikings exist today.

As I wade through all that testosterone, I make the mistake of wondering which of these mounds of muscles is Michael Medvedev. Of course, as soon as I think of Mason's nemesis, I think of the man himself and nearly turn around. But I don't. I keep walking and hop into the nearest cab.

"Where to?" the cabbie asks.

I futilely scan the crowds for any hint of Mason. "Orlando airport."

The cabbie starts the car. "Sounds good."

As the car's engine comes to life, I'm almost sure that Mason will suddenly appear and force me to stay... but that's just wishful thinking.

No romantic deus ex machina for me.

There never is.

I cry all the way to New York.

Chapter 31

Mason

I wake up with an uneasy feeling, and I don't know why.

Well, I kind of do. We'll arrive at the port any moment now, and Sophia and I still haven't discussed our feelings—assuming she has any for me.

Fuck. My strategy to wait until she acknowledges my declaration of love is officially a loser.

Fine. I'll have to talk to her now. Time to put all my cards on the table, or as Coach says: "put the fucking puck on the ice." I can tell her how much I've grown to care for her, and more importantly, what I really think about the imbecilic idea that "what happens on the cruise stays on the cruise."

"Ladybug?" I turn to her side... but find it empty and cold.

What the fuck? Where is she?

"Sophia?" I get up and knock on the bathroom door. No reply.

I try the handle and find the door unlocked.

The bathroom is empty.

My stomach drops. The last few days, we've spent every morning together, so I foolishly assumed today would be the same.

Maybe she's packing?

No. She told me she packed up yesterday.

Maybe she forgot to pack something?

My unease intensifies.

Frantically, I dress, brush my teeth, and run over to knock on Sophia's suite door.

No one answers.

"Ladybug?" I shout, banging my fist on the wood.

No answer.

"Hey," I say to a passing porter. "Open this door."

"I'm sorry, sir," he says, blinking. "If that's not your—"

"I heard a scream inside. Someone might need help."

And hey, it's not a complete lie: if he doesn't do as I say, he will be screaming and in need of help.

"Oh." The porter takes out a keycard and swipes. "Please stay here."

He runs in and I follow, not trusting some stranger to deal with this—whatever it is.

"There's no one here," the porter says, looking around in confusion. "No suitcases either."

No suitcases.

Until this moment, I could've made other guesses, like maybe she went to get some breakfast. But only one explanation fits now: she took her suitcase and left without saying goodbye.

Well, fuck that.

Spinning on my heel, I sprint for the elevator and jab at the button like what's happening is its fault.

The fucking elevator doesn't come for what feels like an hour.

I flip it the bird and sprint for the stairs.

I manage to descend only one level down before I run into a traffic jam of people.

Nope.

I don't care how rude they're about to think I am. Channeling my high school self, I slide down the stair railing to get past the gawking strangers. At the bottom, I run smack into a crowd of passengers waiting to disembark.

Okay. All isn't lost. I'm on the ground level of the ship, and we haven't docked yet. Maybe we can delay docking until I catch her? I take out my phone and dial the captain to call in one last favor.

He doesn't answer.

Fuck.

I call Sophia.

She doesn't answer either. She's either ignoring me on purpose or is still on her "digital detox."

Fine. I start pushing through the crowd.

The ship comes to a halt, and the captain's voice cheerfully slurs about our arrival.

"Let me through," I growl at the people in front of me.

Something in my voice must make them realize that it's best to comply because many people move out of my way, and then I push through the ones who don't.

When I enter the terminal, I spot what could be Sophia's curvy figure hurrying toward the cabs.

I gauge the distance between us.

If this were ice and I had skates on, I'd make it for sure, but as is, I'll have to rely on sprinting.

So, I sprint... and crash into a wall of defensemen that seems to have sprouted from nowhere to block my way.

"What the fuck?"

This seems eerily like a nightmare I sometimes have —though, granted, I'm on the ice naked in that one.

"And hello to you too, Yeti scum," says one of the burly dudes in my way.

I scan them all, and only when I spot a familiar— and unwelcome—face, do I understand.

These are the Florida Bears, a hockey team that isn't our rival but wishes they were.

And, of course, with them is Misha, or rather Michael Medvedev as I'll call him to his face today because I'd rather deescalate the situation than waste valuable seconds kicking everyone's ass.

Is this ambush his idea?

Apart from the usual Soviet-bred discontent on his hawkish face, his expression is unreadable. I've never told him this—as it might sound like a compliment— but he has always reminded me of a bogatyr from Russian folk tales. They are a type of Slavic knights errant and are always depicted as big men fierce enough to slay three-headed dragons.

Oh, and they aren't really team players either.

"Michael," I say, addressing Medvedev directly. "I'm in a big rush. If you care about your teammates' wellbeing, tell them to get out of my fucking way."

Then again, since when does he give two shits about his teammates?

"My wellbeing?" says one of the defensemen, whom I'm going to eviscerate first. "You and what army?"

"Listen," I say in Russian, eyes still only on Medvedev. "I didn't have anything to do with you losing your job. It was Coach's decision, I swear." Not that I didn't agree with said decision, but I didn't help him make it, which is why this isn't a lie.

"Did he just say something about my mama?" grits out the same not-long-for-this-world defenseman. "I'm going to—"

"Shut your mouth," Misha says in perfect, unaccented English, his growly voice carrying so much threat that his teammate swallows the rest of his words. He then turns his attention to me and asks in Russian, "What's in it for me?"

My jaw twitches. "You mean besides avoiding a trip to the hospital?"

He curls his upper lip. "You know perfectly well I could take you alone, if I wished."

"If you wished on a genie lamp, maybe."

He grunts—which for him probably passes for an

amused chuckle. "How about we make a deal," he says, switching to English.

I arch an eyebrow and ball my hand into a fist, just in case.

"A game between our teams," Misha says. "Not as part of the league bullshit. Just for us."

Hmm. "Exhibition game?"

He nods.

"Fine. My team could use the practice." Not that we're going to gain much of that by playing this sorry bunch of Florida Men. Wrestling gators doesn't help you navigate the puck across the ice, nor does punching sharks.

"Move aside," Misha says to his teammates.

They get out of my way, and I sprint to where I saw Sophia.

Except when I get there, there's no sign of her.

Maybe that wasn't her? I search the terminal up and down, but she's nowhere to be found.

Fuck.

On my phone, I pull up the last dispatch I got from Max and check when she's supposed to be flying back to New York.

Okay. Unlike me, who chartered a flight, she is flying first class out of Orlando in two hours. That means I can still intercept her.

Heart hammering, I jump into a cab and bribe the driver to punch it. He does, and the next forty minutes are like a chase scene from *Mission Impossible*... until we hit traffic, that is.

Double fuck.

I tap the driver's shoulder. "Can't you do something?"

He shrugs. "This car doesn't fly. Sorry."

I'm so pissed I want to return to the port and beat up every single player on the Florida Bears team, starting with Misha. Alas, the traffic doesn't let me go forward or backward, and we trudge through it with the speed of one of Sophia's turtles. Or tortoises. Whichever.

Turns out, the cause of the traffic is something that could only happen in Orlando: an off-duty Mickey Mouse drove his beat-up Volkswagen beetle into a BMW.

The driver clears his throat. "I thought Disney employees are forbidden from taking costumes out of the park, let alone wearing them when off duty."

"I guess someone is getting fired today," I say with a sigh.

Once we pass that lovely scene, we get to the airport fast, for all that that's worth. Still, just in case Sophia was late to her flight, I get out and scour the airport for her.

Nope. She's not here.

Fucking fuck.

I take another cab to my private plane, and once I'm in the air, I entertain myself by playing out violent scenarios featuring every member of the Florida Bears, as well as dudes dressed as Mickey Mouse.

Upon landing, I decide that I can't just go home.

Nope. I'm going over to Sophia's mansion.

Hopping into the limo waiting for me, I inform the driver of the change in destination. As we battle yet another bout of traffic, I play out all sorts of conversations in my head. It's not until we're at her gates that I begin to have second thoughts about what I'm doing right now.

After all, her biggest gripe with me was that I was stalking her—and here I go again.

Then again, we have to talk and resolve this.

I can't just let her go.

Wait a second.

Speaking of stalking, there's a guy sitting on the ground just outside the view of Sophia's intercom camera. Seeing him brings to mind the expression "cute as a button," or put another way, he makes me feel disgust and rage.

Oh, and there's something furtive about his position. Something shifty.

Teeth clenching, I exit the car.

The guy spots me, and some sort of recognition seems to spark in his weaselly eyes.

"Who are you?" I demand. "And what the fuck are you doing here?"

I don't care if this isn't my home that he's loitering next to. It's Sophia's, so the fucker had better impress me with his answer.

"You're the hockey player." The guy jumps to his feet and extends his hand toward me. "I'm Rupert."

I look at the proffered appendage as I would at a

pile of blobfish vomit. "I will only ask one more time. What are you doing here?"

He backs up. "I'm here to visit Sophia."

"Why?" If glares could castrate, mine would have him singing contralto.

He flaps his pale lashes, all innocent-like. "She didn't mention me?"

"Why would she?"

Who the fuck is he? She never mentioned a brother, and she said she's never had a serious relationship.

The dude juts out his chest, which makes him look like a pufferfish. "I'm the love of Sophia's life."

I freeze, and for the second time today, I wonder if I'm living a nightmare. Should I pinch myself? No. The sting from my knuckles when they smash into this asshole should suffice.

"You don't believe me?" He pulls out his phone and taps at it. "Here. This is our engagement party."

Feeling like it's he who's punched me, I can't help but check out the image on his screen.

Fuck. There they are, smiling, standing way too close together, and fucking fuck! There's a ring with a microscopic cubic zirconia on Sophia's finger.

Not only was she in a serious relationship, but it was with this shit stain, and... *they were engaged*.

"There are more pics." He swipes at the screen. "For example—"

I snatch his phone and crush it with my fist until the screen cracks. "I'll give you one second to run." I punctuate my words by smashing the phone into the ground.

He stares at it in disbelief, then looks up at me. "What the fuck? That phone was—"

With a satisfying thud, my right fist smashes into what passes for his jaw.

He flies up at least an inch off the ground, then crashes into a heap on the grass.

Shit.

Did I just murder Sophia's ex?

Assuming this is an ex. Maybe they're currently dating, and what happened on the cruise was—

The fucker moans, so I guess he's alive.

"Are you ready to run now?" I growl.

Legs trembling, he gets to his feet and starts to wobble away, silently—proving he's not as suicidal as he seemed at first.

When I can't see him anymore, I turn around—and come face to face with Sophia.

Chapter 32

Sophia

When Effie told me that Mason was by the intercom, it took me all of five seconds to decide to join him—that is how weak I am.

As I run to him, I have no idea what I'll say, but just seeing him will be—

I spot Rupert, and my blood turns into a slushy.

What the fuck is he doing here? I have a restraining order against him at this point—and he's trespassing on top of that.

My heart does a somersault when I realize that he's talking to Mason. Something about his phone.

And then, boom, Mason punches him, and it's like my deepest fantasy came to life, despite my claim of being a pacifist.

"Are you ready to run now?" Mason's tone is so chilling that some part of *me* wants to run as well.

Rupert is not a brave man, so he obviously scrams—

and I get the feeling that I'm finally going to get my wish to never see him again after today.

Mason turns my way, and at first, his eyes light up the way they did every morning on the cruise, but then his expression darkens. "Is what he said true?"

Shit. Rupert said something? "Is what true?"

That the bastard twisted me around his finger? That I thought I was in love and signed whatever he wanted me to sign? That I thought we'd get married and live happily ever after—only to have reality smack me in the face not unlike the way Mason's fist just did to Rupert?

Mason juts an accusing finger at a small pile of phone parts littering the ground. "You were engaged?"

Something inside me snaps. "Sounds like you should get a refund from whoever put together that dossier on me. They missed a major chapter."

Mason's lips press into a razor-thin line. "You don't consider an engagement a serious relationship?"

I feel pressure building behind my eyes, but I fight the urge to cry with every ounce of my free will—which doesn't feel like an illusion at this moment. "You caught me. Now what?"

"I told you about my parents," he says, and there's such pain in his voice that I take a step back.

"And you know how important trust is for me," he continues. "But you didn't tell me about this."

"Why, so you'd know how gullible I really am?" My nostrils flare. "As is, I left the cruise almost ready to sell you your precious team. Wasn't that the goal?"

"Ran from the cruise, you mean?" His gaze turns icy. "Since the day we met, you've always chosen to think the worst of me, yet I've never lied to you." He shakes his head. "I thought there was something between us. Something real. Something special."

I take a step back. "How could I be sure that you weren't with me because you still wanted the team?" This question is directed at both of us... maybe more at myself than at him.

Mason's features turn thunderous. "If I were as bad a person as you always assume, and if I wanted the team *that* badly, I could just say, 'Sell, or your friend doesn't get the job of her dreams.'"

I stagger back, and I'm pretty sure I know how Rupert must've felt a minute ago. "Are you threatening me?"

He turns on his heel. "Take it as you wish."

With that, he strides over to his limo, bangs its door shut so hard it will need repair, and with a screech of tires, he's gone.

Chapter 33

Sophia

I don't recall how I get back into the mansion. Mind in complete disarray, I shamble over to visit Donatello and April—the hope being that their grazing might soothe my mind.

Bad idea. They're humping, which painfully reminds me of my favorite activity involving Mason.

"Is everything okay?" Dr. Kelpcon asks.

Wow. How bad must I look that the good doctor is able to focus on me instead of her favorite charges mid-coitus?

"I'm fine." The lie of the century. "I'm going to go inside."

I do that, then pace the mansion like a captive, my mind replaying the entirety of the cruise and the most recent encounter with Mason on a torturous loop.

"I thought there was something between us," he'd said. "Something real. Something special."

At the time that he said those words, I wasn't fully

listening, but now it's all I can think about because they feel so true.

What happened between us felt like more than just a guy trying to get something from me.

It felt like something real.

Felt like love… at least for me.

But that's the problem. I thought I loved Rupert too, and look what happened.

In hindsight, I don't think what I felt for Rupert was love. It was simply that I was craving love after Mom's betrayal, and I stupidly thought he might provide it. At most, what Rupert and I had was a friendship with some infatuation on my end.

With Mason, it's entirely different. It has been from the first moment we met. Maybe that's why I felt so hostile toward him. It wasn't just the brief conversation I overheard. It was him. I felt the threat to my heart, and I put up my shields. Shields that didn't hold.

Despite all the care I took to nurture my defenses, Mason managed to penetrate them—and I should've known he could.

He is so fucking good at penetration in general.

I halt in my tracks.

Did I just admit to myself that I love Mason?

Yes. I did. Because I do, despite the fact that he threatened Abigail's job.

No. Not despite that. I simply don't believe that he would do that.

But what if he does?

I should at least warn Abigail of the possibility.

Taking my phone out, I try calling her, but then I realize it's still in airplane mode.

Crap.

As soon as I disable said mode, a flood of missed calls, texts, and emails arrives—mostly from Mason in regard to my sudden departure from the cruise.

Oh, and tellingly, there are zero after the conversation we just had.

My stomach sinking, I call Abigail.

"Hey," she says. "Are you back? I've been trying to reach you."

"Yeah. Just got back. I wanted—"

"No, me first," she chirps excitedly. "I've got the job. Thank you! Thank you! Thank you!"

My chest squeezes. Abigail's already gotten the job. And Mason must've known this—but he didn't use the information to his advantage, just like he never brought up delaying the cruise ship when I was seasick.

"You there?" Abigail asks.

"Yeah. I'm happy for you," I say. "It's just that... I think I fucked up. Big."

"What happened?"

I tell her, and when I finish, she confirms what I already thought: Mason must have known she got the job for at least two days now, via his friend, which means what I interpreted as a threat was simply a point Mason tried to make.

"Can't he get you fired?" I ask, but I don't believe that anymore.

"Extremely unlikely," she says. "For starters, when

you join Octothorpe, you get shares in the company as a sign-on bonus—and they cost a fortune. If they terminated me for no reason at all, I'd get to keep those. Furthermore—"

"I've got to fix this," I say, more to myself than to her.

"Yes, you do," she says sternly. "Now go and do that. We'll talk after."

I hang up and dial Mr. Cohen to make the necessary arrangements before telling Richard to get my fastest car ready.

I'm going to Mason's place, and I'm going to make this right.

Chapter 34

Mason

When I storm into my apartment, both Spike and the cat sitter I hired to look after him examine me with similarly worried expressions.

I pay the woman and relieve her of her duties, then soothingly stroke Spike's fur—the soothing more for me than for him. After a while, my anger has cooled to the point where I want to go back and explain to Sophia that I'd never torpedo her friend's job, not that it's even possible now that she's been hired.

But no.

Sophia won't open the gates for me. Or talk to me again.

Fucking fuck. I was so jealous after meeting her ex I couldn't control my big mouth.

Then again, I don't care if she doesn't open the gates. I'm heading back there. If I don't set the record straight, I—

My phone rings.

It's Cohen.

I don't have time for lawyers right now, so I ignore it... except he calls again. And again.

"What?" I bark into the phone.

He informs me that Sophia is selling me the team, and for a pittance.

"No," I say. "Not if this means we're never going to see each other again."

He clears his throat. "The day I start giving my clients relationship advice is the day I'm going to burn my law degree."

"I wasn't... never mind. I've got to go." I hang up and rush outside to hail a cab.

Suddenly, a Bugatti Bolide comes to a screeching halt next to the sidewalk.

I gape as Sophia emerges from it, her brown eyes zeroed in on me.

"Hi," I say stupidly.

"Hi," she replies.

"I'm sorry," we say in unison, and then we just stand there, staring at each other.

The way my heart is hammering in my chest, you'd think I've just gone through the whole rink on a single breath and scored a goal. What is Sophia thinking? Is her mind in the same kind of turmoil as mine?

I clear my throat. "Ladies first? Or is it more gentlemanly for me to explain myself?"

She swallows. "I'm not sure where to even start."

"Well, I do." I take a deep breath. "I'm sorry if it sounded like I was threatening Abigail's dream job. I would never do that, no matter what happens to the team, or between us."

Sophia bites her lip. "I'm sorry about that too. I didn't think you would... after I gave it a second of thought, that is. That's just not like you."

"Thank you."

I'm not even sure if I agree that getting the team no matter the cost is "not like me." It's just that I wouldn't do something like that if Sophia was in any way involved.

"You're welcome." She steps closer. "I shouldn't have run from the cruise. And I should've told you about Rupert—or at least said something like, 'I had a shitty long-term relationship and don't want to talk about it.'"

When I hear the fucker's name, my fists clench and unclench, a gesture she clearly notices, judging by the way her gaze flicks to my hands.

I do my best to relax them. "I understand why you didn't." At least I *think* I do. "He hurt you."

"It's not just that. I was stupid. And gullible. I let myself be used and—"

I clasp her shoulders. "You don't have to go into it right now if you don't want to," I say softly. "You can tell me whenever you're ready. Or not tell me at all. It's up to you."

And what she says or doesn't say will determine just how many of the fucker's bones I will break. But that's a decision for later.

Her eyes gleam brighter. "Okay. But again, I *am* sorry. And I shouldn't have assumed the worst of—"

I stop her with a kiss. One that continues in the elevator to my apartment and culminates in a long, steamy session in my bedroom.

We're still wrapped around each other when a jungle creature pounces on my feet and nibbles playfully on my toes.

"Spike!" I say sternly, untangling myself from Sophia to sit up and give my cat a glare.

He gives me the most innocent look ever and strolls over the blankets to Sophia to give her chin a furry rub —the ultimate feline complement. Grinning, she pets him, and a rush of warm emotions overwhelms me.

This feels so right, having her here at my place, playing with my cat in my bed. This is where she belongs... with me. Forever.

Sophia is still petting Spike when her gaze catches mine, her expression peculiarly uncertain. "So... there's something you said in Jamaica that I wanted to talk to you about... That, and when you said that there was something between us. Something real. Something special."

My heart picks up its pace again. "You mean when I told you how I feel about you?"

She sucks in a breath. "So... you were talking to *me*?"

I stare at her. "Who else?"

She shrugs, Socrates and Plato bobbing up and down so temptingly that Uber receives a fresh surge of blood. "You did telepathically communicate with a dolphin earlier that very day."

Did I? Oh, shit. I guess I did. Like that one amazing idea I had that day, the dolphin telepathy totally slipped my mind. But not my declaration to Sophia.

That I would never forget.

"I was definitely talking to you," I say as Spike loses interest in us in favor of sharpening his claws on my pillow. Chunks of memory foam fly my way, but I ignore them because Sophia's eyes shine brighter at my words.

"So it wasn't the pot talking?" she confirms.

"Definitely not."

She bites her lip, tempting me again. "And now that the team is yours, do you feel the same way?"

I clasp her hands in mine. "Yes, Ladybug. I love you. I love you more with each passing day. I love you more than I could ever love a dolphin. Or a killer whale, which, according to a nature documentary I saw recently, is actually a type of dolphin."

She grins. "Me too. I love you, that is. And no dolphin can compare to you either. Not even a dolphin who happens to be a philosopher. Or a Viking. But if I ever met a Viking philosopher dolphin, then—"

I silence her with another kiss.

Epilogue

Sophia

I look toward Donatello and April as they step down from the ship onto what has recently been renamed TMNT Island, at least until a cease-and-decease letter makes its new owner rename it to something that isn't trademarked.

"Do you think they know how momentous this occasion is?" I ask no one in particular.

April's answer is to munch on some nearby dune grass, ignoring the rest of the gorgeous wild beach in front of her.

"Doubt it." Mason slips on his backpack and strolls onto the beach like he owns the place—which as of recently, he does. The beach and the whole island.

"Of course, they know this is a big day," Dr. Kelpcon counters. "They're about to rejoin the offspring they've been diligently creating as saviors of their species."

Ignoring the grass, Donatello gets into his all-too-familiar position behind April.

"Huh," I say. "Doesn't look like Don thinks the species has been sufficiently saved."

As the humping commences, Dr. Kelpcon can't resist giving the tortoises her usual pointers, and like at home, Mason and I leave her to it, in this case by going to explore the rest of the island.

"Want to check out Splinter's Lagoon?" Mason asks. "Or the Gulf of Shredder?"

I sigh. "Whoever owns *Teenage Mutant Ninja Turtles* is going to make you rename all of those landmarks, you know that, right?"

He shrugs. "The lagoon is named for the splinters you get if you dare climb the palm trees, not after the wise rat sensei who trained certain turtles."

I roll my eyes. "What about Shredder?"

"I've gone paperless recently, and this gulf celebrates the retirement of my favorite paper shredder."

"Let me guess," I say. "TMNT really stands for The Mighty Nighttime Troupe?"

"Yeah," he says. "The best burlesque in the world."

I shake my head. "Do you think it's weird that I'm jealous of a fictional performance where you might see scantily clad women?"

He snorts. "I never said the burlesque show would feature women."

"Ah, what was I thinking? It's probably sexy tortoises all the way down."

"Bingo," he says. "Now... the lagoon?"

"Sure." We walk to said location and then sit on a

bench overlooking the ocean as one of Donatello's children crosses our path.

Okay. I'd better tell Mason what's going on. But how is he going to react? I guess there's one way to find out.

I inhale the salty air for courage. "There's something I wanted to talk to you about."

Mason turns away from the view and looks into my eyes, which never fails to animate the ladybugs in my belly.

"What's going on? A problem with the sabbatical?"

"No. The school got someone to cover for me." I drag in another breath. "What I have to say, like this whole trip, has to do with continuing a species. In this case, they're the opposite of extinct but—"

"You're pregnant?" He leaps to his feet.

Shit. Is he upset? Why else would—

He drags me to my feet and envelops me in a muscly bear hug.

"This is amazing!" he shouts into my ear.

Then, letting go of me, he asks the question that I had to answer for myself when I noticed that Aunt Flo never came to visit. "How?"

"Turns out, antibiotics and birth control pills don't play well together," I say.

Yes, somehow, I didn't know this, though I *do* know what "acosmism" means. Just shows you how practical a philosophy degree is.

Mason beams at me. "Do you know if it's a boy or a girl?"

Is it possible to tell this early? I guess I'm not the only one who doesn't know the basics of human procreation. "The line on the pee stick looked a little bit like a hockey stick. So… maybe a boy?"

The only other time I've seen such an expression of wonder on Mason's face was while watching his favorite nature documentary. "Girls can play hockey too. Either way, incredible."

"Yeah." It really will be.

"Well, then, I have something to talk to you about as well." He rummages in his backpack until he pulls out a small black box.

My eyes widen. "Is that…?"

He drops to one knee. "The original plan was to do this on the cliffs of Møns Klint, during our trip to Denmark, but if hockey has taught me anything, it's how to adapt."

Rendered speechless, I stare down at him and just nod.

"Ladybug," Mason continues, his gray eyes gleaming. "You're the love of my life, and now you will be the mother of my child. Would you do me the greatest honor and marry me?" He opens the box, revealing a giant diamond set in a band that resembles a sword.

My power of speech partially returns, enabling me to ask, "What's with the stabby-stabby?" I point at the band.

Mason gives me a wide smile. "Vikings exchanged swords as part of *their* wedding ceremony, so I figured we could use one as part of our engagement too."

"Wow!" Denmark and Viking wedding rituals? The man has a whole theme in mind. I almost squeal out loud, but then moderate my response to a more temperate, "Thank you! It's awesome."

Mason narrows his eyes. "Aren't you forgetting a small little formality?"

"Ah, right." I grab the ring and put it on my ring finger. "Yes, Mason, I'll marry you... under one condition."

"Name it," he says solemnly.

I'm so giddy with excitement my knees wobble. "I want to keep my maiden name."

"Oh?"

I give him a big grin. "I'm having way too much fun watching my students' discomfort when they try to address me as Professor Papachristodoulopoulou."

Mason laughs and rises to his feet. "You got it." He glances at my belly and cocks his head. "What about the baby? I doubt growing up with your last name was all that fun."

"Good point," I say. "Which is why the little one shall be a Tugev."

"That works." He clasps my hands in his. "Now we have to celebrate."

Huh. "The last time we celebrated, you got me preggers."

"That just means I can't get you *more* preggers."

Mason pulls me to him for a kiss that spells the beginning of a celebration that will last the rest of today—and tonight.

And likely the rest of our lives.

Sneak Peeks

Thank you for participating in Sophia and Mason's journey!

Ready for more hot billionaires? Check out *Billionaire Grump*, a fake relationship romcom about a sharp-tongued aspiring botanist, a sexy, Ancient Rome-obsessed grump, and one fateful encounter in an elevator that goes hilariously wrong.

Love vacation romances? Read *Billionaire Surfer*! It follows Brooklyn, an overworked single mom in desperate need of a vacation, and Evan, a billionaire surfer who, like the ocean waves, might just sweep Brooklyn off of her feet.

To make sure you never miss a release, sign up for the newsletter at <u>mishabell.com</u>.

Turn the page to read previews from *Billionaire Grump* and *Billionaire Surfer*!

Excerpt from Billionaire Grump

By Misha Bell

Juno

When I'm late for a job interview and get stuck on an elevator with an annoyingly sexy, Ancient Rome-obsessed grump, the last thing I expect is for him to be the billionaire owner of the building. I also don't expect to almost kill him… accidentally, of course.

Sure, I don't get the plant care position I applied for, but I do receive an interesting offer.

Lucius needs to trick the public (and his grandma) into thinking he's in a relationship, and I need tuition money to get my botany degree. Our arrangement is mutually beneficial—that is, until I start catching feelings.

If being a cactus lover has taught me anything, it's that

if you get too close, there's a good chance you'll end up hurt.

Lucius

Post-elevator incident, I'm left with three things: my favorite water bottle full of pee, a life threatening allergic reaction, and paparazzi photos of my "girlfriend" and I that make my Gram the happiest woman alive.

Naturally, my next step is to blackmail—I mean, convince—this (admittedly cute) girl to pretend to date me. That way, my grandma stays happy, and as a bonus, I can keep the gold diggers at bay.

Unfortunately, my arch nemesis, a.k.a. biology, kicks in, and the whole "not getting physical" part of our agreement becomes increasingly hard to abide by. Worse yet, the longer I'm with Juno, the more my delicately crafted icy exterior melts away.

If I'm not careful, Juno will tear down my walls completely.

———

"Are you calling me stupid?" I snap. Anyone could have trouble with these damn buttons, not just a person with dyslexia.

He looks pointedly at the buttons. "Stupid is as stupid does."

I grind my teeth, painfully. "You're an asshole. And you've watched *Forrest Gump* one too many times."

His lips flatten. "That movie wasn't the origin of that saying. It's from Latin: *Stultus est sicut stultus facit*."

I roll my eyes. "What kind of pretentious *stultus* quotes Latin?"

The steel in his eyes is so cold I bet my tongue would get stuck if I tried to lick his eyeball. "I don't know. Maybe the 'idiot' who happens to like everything related to Rome, including their numerals."

My jaw drops open. "You made this decision?" I wave toward the elevator buttons.

He nods.

Shit. He probably heard me earlier, which means I started the insults. In my defense, he did make an idiotic choice.

I exhale a frustrated breath. "If you're such an expert on Roman numerals, you could've told me which one to press."

He crosses his arms over his chest. "You didn't ask me."

My hackles rise again. "Ask you? You looked like you might bite my head off for just existing."

"That's because you delayed—"

The elevator jerks to a stop, and the lights around us dim.

We both stare at the doors.

They stay shut.

He turns to me and narrows his eyes accusingly. "What did you press now?"

"Me? How? I've been facing you. Unfortunately."

With an annoying headshake, he stalks toward the panel with the buttons, and I have to leap away before I get trampled.

"You probably pressed something earlier," he mutters. "Why else would we be stuck?"

Why is it illegal to choke people? Just a few seconds with my hands on his throat would be a calming exercise.

Instead, I glare at his back, which is blocking my view of what he's doing, if anything. "The poor elevator probably just committed suicide over these Roman numerals. It knew that when someone sees things like L and XL, they think of T-shirt sizes for Neanderthal types like you. And don't get me started on that XXX button, which is a clear reference to porn. It creates a hostile work env—"

"Can you shut up so I can get us out of this?" he snaps.

His words bring home the reality of our situation: it's been over a minute, and the doors are still closed.

Dear saguaro, am I really stuck here? With this guy? What about my interview?

"Silence, finally," he says with satisfaction and moves to the side, so I see him jam his finger at the "help" button.

"It's a miracle that's not in Latin," I can't help but say. "Or Klingon."

"Hello?" he says into the speaker under the button, his voice dripping with irritation.

No reply, not even static.

"Anyone there?" His annoyance is clearly rising to new heights. "I'm late for an important meeting."

"And I'm late for an interview," I chime in, in case it matters.

He pauses to arch a thick eyebrow at me. "An interview? For what position?"

I stand straighter. "I'm sure the likes of you don't realize this, but the plants in this building don't take care of themselves."

Wait. Have I said too much? Could he torpedo my interview—assuming this elevator snafu hasn't done it already? What does he do here, anyway—design ridiculous elevators? That can't be a full-time job, can it?

"A tree hugger," he mutters under his breath. "That tracks."

What an asshole. I've never hugged a tree in my life. I'm too busy talking to them.

He returns his scowling attention to the "help" button—though now I'm thinking it should've been labeled as "no help."

"Hello? Can you hear me?" he shouts. "Answer now, or you're fired."

I roll my eyes. "Is it a good idea to be a dick to the person who can save us?"

He blows out an audible breath. "It doesn't matter.

The button must be malfunctioning. They wouldn't dare ignore me."

I pull out my trusty phone, a nice and simple Nokia 3310. "Full of yourself much?"

He stares at my hands incredulously. "So that's why the elevator got stuck. It went through a time warp and transported us to 2008."

I frown at the lack of reception on my Nokia. "This version was released in 2017."

"It still looks dumber than a brain-dead crash test dummy." He proudly pulls an iPhone from his pocket. "*This* is what a phone should look like."

I scoff. "That's what constant distraction looks like. Anyway, if your iNotSoSmartPhone—trademarked—is so great, it should have some reception, right?"

He glances at his screen, but I can tell he already knows the truth: no reception for his darling either.

Still, I can't resist. "See? Your genius of a phone is just as useless. All it's good for is turning people into social-media-checking zombies."

He hides the device, like a protective parent. "On top of all your endearing qualities, you're a technophobe too?"

I debate throwing my Nokia at his head but decide it's not worth shelling out sixty-five bucks for a replacement. "Just because I don't want to be distracted doesn't mean I'm a technophobe."

"Actually, my phone is great at blocking out distractions." He puts the headphones back over his ears. "See?" He presses play, and I hear the faint riffs of heavy metal.

"Very mature," I mouth at him.

"Sorry," he says overly loudly. "I can't hear any distractions."

Fine. Whatever. At least he has good taste in music. My cactus and I are big fans of Metallica, which is what I think he's listening to.

I begin to pace back and forth.

I'm stuck, and I'm late. If this elevator jam doesn't resolve itself in the next minute or two, I can pretty much kiss the new job goodbye—and by extension, my tuition money. No tuition money means no botany degree, which has been my dream for the last few years.

By saguaro's juices, this sucks really bad.

I sneak a glance at the hottie—I mean, asshole.

What would he say about someone with dyslexia wanting a college degree? Probably that I'd need a university that uses coloring books. In truth, even coloring books wouldn't help that much—I can never stay inside those stupid lines.

I sigh and look away, increasingly worried. My dreams aside, what if the elevator stays stuck for a while?

The most immediate problem is my growing need to pee—but paradoxically, a longer-term worry will be finding liquids to drink.

I wonder... If you're thirsty enough, does your body reabsorb the water from the bladder? Also, could I

MacGyver a filter to reclaim the water in my urine with what I have on me? Maybe through cat hair?

I shiver, and only partially from the insane AC that's somehow reaching me even in here. In the short term, it would be so much better if it were hot instead of cold. I'd sweat out the liquids and not need to pee, though I guess I'd die of thirst sooner. I sneak an envious glance at the large stranger. I bet he has a bladder the size of a blimp. He also has a stainless-steel bottle that's probably filled with water that he likely won't share.

There's also the question of food. I don't have anything edible with me, apart from a can of cat food... and, theoretically, the cat herself.

No. I'd sooner eat this stranger than poor Atonic.

As if psychic, the stranger's stomach growls.

Crap. With this guy being so big and mean, he'd probably eat the cat. After that, he'd eat me... and not in a fun way.

I'm so, so screwed.

———

Visit <u>www.mishabell.com</u> to order your copy of *Billionaire Grump* today!

Excerpt from Billionaire Surfer
By Misha Bell

An overworked single mom from New York City. A billionaire surfer from Florida. Can the turn of the tide bring these two together?

Brooklyn
Ah, finally a vacation. My son is at summer camp. My worries are back in the city. Now I just get to sit back, relax, and... get into a heated argument with my Airbnb host? Speaking of heat, is the Florida sun getting to my head, or is it the drop-dead gorgeous man in front me?

My friends did say I need some *Vitamin D*...

But my life is complicated, and no amount of adventure-filled treasure hunting, steamy make-out sessions, or ocean-deep conversations can convince me that our beach affair could last. Especially once Evan learns my secret.

Evan

I'm rich on paper, but I don't live my life like a typical billionaire. Nor do I date tourists. Especially ones who mistake me for a plumber and eat my breakfast before I have a chance to quell my hanger.

Brooklyn is argumentative, rude, stubborn, beautiful, smart, fun... Okay, let's say I kind of like her. That doesn't change the fact that she's only here for a week —or that I haven't told her an important fact about myself.

But if surfing has taught me anything, it's that you have to seize the moment before it's gone. And what if I don't want to let her go?

———

On the flight to Jacksonville, Reagan plays his video game while I do my best not to snap at him or any other innocent bystanders. Thanks to my shit luck, the Red Wedding arrived mere hours ago, giving me the kind of cramps that, if you gave them to a prisoner of war, would go against the Geneva Conventions.

Thanks, body. Was a relaxing plane ride too much to ask for?

I glare at my wrist where my birthday gift from last year resides. It's an Octothorpe Glorp, a fitness tracker that's supposed to warn me when Aunt Flo is coming to town. Often, I imagine the gizmo talking back to me in a voice that's a mix of Richard Simmons and Gollum:

My dear Precious, if I could, I'd keep every tampon you've ever used in a shrine and glue to them the smiles I cut out of my favorite pictures of you. Alas, when it comes to the feature you mention, I merely track your cycles, not predict them.

I suffer the rest of the flight as stoically as I can. Once we land, I rent a car and drive Reagan straight to the camp—a beachy and chill establishment that plays Jimmy Buffett on a loop.

"Okay, bye," Reagan says without a second of hesitation before running off to check the place out.

I wait to make sure he doesn't run back and tell me he doesn't like what he sees. Nope. He probably thinks I've already left, or has forgotten that I exist altogether.

"He'll have access to a phone," the nearest Boy-Scout-looking counselor says to me reassuringly. "And we have your number on file. Once he's settled in, he'll give you a call. Go."

With a sigh, I head back to the car and start driving.

My mood was already crummy, but now it's worse than that of a stressed-out, sleep-deprived, and tick-riddled hippopotamus. The green and idyllic nature around me only makes me feel shitty about where I actually live, as do the much nicer roads and cleaner streets. But then I almost run over an-honest-to-goodness live alligator and feel a little better about the comparison between my namesake in NYC and Palm Islet, Florida, the illustrious little town where my vacation is to be. Same goes when a deer tries to commit suicide by car a few minutes later, and when the woman in the car in front of me stops to rescue a turtle—getting peed on in the process.

Got to love Florida.

My Airbnb turns out to be located in a gated community, and the female security guard at the entrance is as thorough as a TSA officer. When all my papers seem to be in order, she wrinkles her nose and mutters something about the HOA usually prohibiting Airbnb rentals in the community, and that mine is a rare exception to the rule. She further informs me that the HOA usually charges an overnight guest fee, but that the owner of *my* Airbnb is exempt from "all the rules."

Oh, the humanity. How do the poor members of the HOA sleep at night? As I drive away, it takes effort not to ask if the HOA in this case stands for Hilariously Overbearing Authority.

Driving through the community, I notice that the houses are charming mixes of Spanish, Mediterranean, and Caribbean styles, and that they all have impeccable lawns—must be the same HOA ruling with an iron fist. But when I pull into the cul-de-sac where my Airbnb is located, the monotone pattern is broken. Houses number four and five on Gatorview Drive are twins, and both have sharp corners, are covered in mirrored surfaces and tons of chrome, and remind me of something you might see in a modern art museum.

Since one of these is mine, I assume both belong to the same HOA rules-exempt owner.

My mood lifts minutely as I spot the lake adjacent to both houses, with untouched nature on the opposite bank. The view from my Airbnb must be spectacular, though slightly less so than from the neighboring house.

I check my fitness tracker for the time.

Dearest Precious ought to consider taking more steps, to tighten those succulent thighs for my stalking—I mean viewing—pleasure.

Crap. I'm too early for check in, and it's getting pretty hot. According to Evan, who's been sending me taciturn texts on behalf of this Airbnb, the code for the garage lock can only be used after eleven-thirty, but I may die of heatstroke by then.

Also, I kind of want the vacation to start, along with the associated relaxation.

Why don't I test said code now?

Walking up to the garage, I type in the code and the door opens. Score! Between this and the lack of a car in the driveway or in the garage, I'm pretty sure I can get inside the house.

After parking in the garage, I open the door to the house proper—which, according to Evan, is the entrance I'll use to come and go.

The door leads right into an ultra-modern kitchen the size of my whole apartment, and there, on the granite island, stands a spread of yummy tapas.

Now this is a fancy welcome. I spot a tiny piece of

grilled salmon, a giant bean, a side of rice, an assortment of pickles, a ton of tiny vegetable plates, and something that looks and smells just like miso soup.

Japanese tapas?

Shrugging, I taste the salmon as I take in the lake view through a floor-to-ceiling window.

I'm jealous of Floridians yet again. In New York, you'd have to be a billionaire to have anything close to this house with this kind of view.

The fish is divine, so I sample each of the veggies, which are also amazing. Even the bean is tasty, and the miso soup is the best of its kind, sweet and savory in equal measure.

Suddenly, I hear rustling on the other side of the island.

What the hell?

The island is blocking my view, so I gingerly step over to where the sound is coming from—a sink that I couldn't see earlier.

I gasp.

A man is getting to his feet. Based on the tools scattered on the floor, I assume he must be a plumber here to fix said sink.

Now I'll admit, until today, if I were forced to picture a plumber in my head, he (is that sexist?) would look like Super Mario with a cartoonish mustache, coveralls, and as much sex appeal as a blobfish.

This plumber, however, has to be the hottest man I've ever seen.

His eyes are the clear blue of a Siberian Husky, his hair is the sun-bleached shade of a Golden Retriever's coat, and his sharp angular facial features are godlike with no dog analogs. Sadly, his ears are covered by headphones, but I bet they are sexy too. Oh, and his bare chest boasts an army of glistening muscles that include a six pack. Also, his nipples are hard.

Correction, it's *my* nipples that are hard.

Spotting me, he frowns, but he makes even grumpy look good. Then his gaze falls on what remains of the tapas, and his eyes beam icicles at me.

"Who are you?" he demands in a low growl that somehow manages to be sexy. "And why did you eat my fucking breakfast?"

Visit www.mishabell.com to order your copy of *Billionaire Surfer* today!